# HIDDEN IDENTITY

Janet Lister was amazed when the secretarial agency offered her the job of personal assistant to the best-selling romantic fiction author Carla Ryder. But she found that Carla's villa on the Greek island of Spetse was filled with mysteries — not least of all the handsome Paul Stavropolous. Janet was sure she recognised Paul, but he couldn't, or wouldn't, explain why. What was the secret everyone in the villa seemed determined to keep from her?

BRENDA LACEY

# HIDDEN IDENTITY

*Complete and Unabridged*

**LINFORD**
*Leicester*

First published in Great Britain

First Linford Edition
published 1999

Copyright © 1994 by Brenda Lacey

British Library CIP Data

Lacey, Brenda
  Hidden identity.—Large print ed.—
Linford romance library
  1. Love stories
  2. Large type books
  I. Title
  823.9′14 [F]

  ISBN 0–7089–5614–9

Published by
F. A. Thorpe (Publishing) Ltd.
Anstey, Leicestershire

Set by Words & Graphics Ltd.
Anstey, Leicestershire
Printed and bound in Great Britain by
T. J. International Ltd., Padstow, Cornwall

This book is printed on acid-free paper

# 1

Janet raised her head, braving the London drizzle, and looked at her reflection in the plate-glass doors of Placewell Secretarial Services Inc. She sighed at what she saw. The tight plait, instead of sitting neatly at the nape of her neck, was escaping into lank, wet wisps. The big, unnecessary spectacles, bought to make her young face look more efficient, had slid down the upturned nose and hid the wide, brown eyes behind rain-splattered lenses. Her best, dark-grey coat had been a bargain, but even Janet had to admit it was several sizes too big.

She pushed open the door. The blonde girl seated behind the desk didn't even look up.

'Good-morning.' Janet said into the silence. The girl went on chewing gum. 'I've come to enquire — '

1

'Name?' the girl demanded through the gum. Her bright-pink lips hardly moved as she spoke.

'Janet,' Janet said. 'Janet Lister.'

The girl raised a pair of lilac-lidded eyes and looked at the computer screen. 'Lister, Janet, secretary. Top Flat, twenty seven A, Priory Road. That the one?'

'Yes.'

'Hmm. Fair shorthand, good typing. We placed you with Cambay and Son six months ago. What happened to that?'

Janet said nothing. Cambay and Son had been a wonderful firm to work for. Old Mr Cambay had been a considerate boss, but the 'and Son' still brought a lump to Janet's throat. She had spent six months trying to forget the blue eyes and treacherous smile of David Cambay. Don't ask any more, she prayed inwardly. Don't ask why I left Cambay's.

The blonde girl didn't ask. She said, 'There's not much about. Have you

2

worked with a word processor?'

'I could learn,' Janet said, without much hope.

The girl smiled. The smile was more discouraging than any words. She gave a list of possible appointments. She was right. There wasn't much about.

Janet began to take down details of some of the less unattractive jobs. Suddenly the telephone shrilled. The pink-nailed fingers seized it.

'Placewell Secretarial, good-morning. Ah, yes, Mr Trout. No, I'm afraid we haven't yet . . . it is very short notice . . . unless . . . ' She looked at Janet. 'Perhaps we can find you someone after all, Mr Trout. Could you ring back in ten minutes?'

She replaced the receiver. 'You may be in luck.' She fumbled through a pile of notes on her desk. 'You prepared to work outside London?'

Janet gulped, remembering David. 'Yes,' she said, 'quite prepared.'

'Got a passport?'

'Passport?' Janet echoed foolishly.

3

'Yes. Why do I need a passport?'

The blonde girl ignored the question. 'And can you look after yourself? Do your own washing, that sort of thing?'

'Well, naturally,' Janet said, wondering what sort of secretary would expect to have her washing done for her.

'Well, then, this might suit you.' She looked at Janet enquiringly. 'Any ties?'

'No ties.' Janet thought of David Cambay, of her cheerless bedsit with the faded wallpaper. 'No,' she said again, 'definitely no ties.'

'One thing,' the girl went on, looking at her notes. 'The person we need must be fairly — oh, no, that's just a note to us.'

'Fairly what?' Janet wanted to know.

'Fairly — able to look after themselves,' the girl said lamely. 'And the pay is excellent. Half as much again as you were getting at Cambay's. And you get your keep, on top.'

Janet wanted to ask a thousand questions. Why, if she was to look after herself, did the job offer her her keep? Why did she need a passport? What did that note really say? She contented herself with asking, 'What kind of business is it? And who is Mr Trout?'

'Well, it isn't exactly a business. It's some woman who's a writer. Mr Trout is her agent. Some woman called —' She consulted the note on her computer again. 'Carla Ryder.'

'Carla Ryder?' Janet repeated in a strangled voice.

The girl looked at her in puzzlement. 'You've heard of her?'

'I should say so.' It seemed astonishing that anyone could not have heard of Carla Ryder. Her books of romantic fiction were bestsellers in a dozen languages. She had been on a TV programme once, escorted by the most handsome man Janet had ever seen. Even now, years later, there were photographs of her in the gossip pages, a new man on her arm in every picture. The perfect figure, the mane of red hair, and the cool, green eyes . . . oh, yes, Janet had heard of Carla Ryder. 'She's very famous.'

'I wouldn't know,' the blonde girl said. 'Anyway, she's looking for a new personal assistant. Apparently the last one left in a hurry. Sacked, I gather. She wants another one urgently. And, as I say, the pay's good.'

The figure she named made Janet whistle. 'She could get anyone for that money.'

'Not by tomorrow, she couldn't. Most people just can't go all that distance, at the drop of a hat.'

Janet was trying to imagine a writer's life. France, perhaps? Italy? 'Where, exactly?'

'Oh, didn't I tell you?' the blonde girl said. She began filing her fingernails. 'She wants someone to go to Somerset tomorrow, and then to Greece on Friday.' The telephone rang again. 'I understand she isn't exactly easy to work for.' She picked up the receiver.

'Tell her I'll take it,' Janet said.

* * *

Janet arrived at Ryder Hall shortly after
ten the next morning. It was a huge,
rambling, country house, of golden
brick, whose rolling lawns made Janet
feel quite overawed. She climbed out
of her little car, and up the imposing,
stone steps, almost too nervous to rap
the door with the brass, lion's-head
knocker.

The door opened, and a tall, youngish
man with auburn hair was looking at
her enquiringly.

She had half-expected to find some
elderly retainer, all dressed in black.
This athletic figure in sweatshirt and
jeans came as rather a surprise. She
blushed. 'I'm Janet. Janet Lister.
Placewell Secretarial Agency.'

'Steve Trout.' He extended a hand.
'We've been expecting you. Have you
come far?'

'London,' Janet said.

'This morning? You must have left
early. Have you eaten?'

She hadn't, of course. The cup of coffee in her flat at five that morning seemed a long time ago. She shook her head.

'Well, come on in,' he said. 'I don't know what there is in the house, but I'm sure we'll find you something. This way.' He led the way down a large, panelled hall, and gestured vaguely at the packing cases stacked against the walls. 'Excuse the mess,' he said cheerfully. 'We're a bit at sixes and sevens.' He pushed open a heavy door. 'In here,' he said.

The room was clearly a study. The big desk was covered in telephones. There was a chaise-longue, and Janet's feet were sinking deep into a luxurious carpet. Every surface, from floor to window-ledge, was covered in a drift of papers. Ashtrays overflowed with half-smoked cigarettes, and pieces of card littered the desk. The impression was of breathtaking untidiness. Janet gasped. Steve Trout gave her an amused look.

'A bit daunting, isn't it?' he said,

not unkindly. 'What you are looking at is the manuscript of 'Soft Sands at Sunset.' We have until Friday.'

Janet's eyes swept over the tumbled piles of paper. 'That's quite an undertaking.'

Steve nodded. 'It certainly is. Carla's last secretary made a start, but as you see — '

Janet took the plunge. 'Her last secretary. Yes. Why did she leave?' The question, once it was asked, seemed awfully rude, and she blundered on. 'I mean, I can't imagine why anyone would leave like that, with a trip to Greece and everything — '

Steve shot her a questioning look. 'That seems very attractive, does it? Have you been to Greece before?'

'No, I've only been abroad the once. Just for a fortnight to get over a broken heart. To tell you the truth, that's why I wanted another job. To get away and have a new start. Without men! Oh, I'm sorry,' she said, 'I didn't mean — '

9

Steve was laughing. 'No, don't apologise. I'm sincerely glad to hear it. That was really the problem with the last secretary. She spent her whole time in Greece flirting with the local young men. It wasn't satisfactory. A woman in Carla's position needs a secretary who is quiet and discreet.'

'I don't think you'll need to worry about me,' Janet said.

Steve laughed. 'I'm sure you'll be splendid. Always supposing that you can type. And are you any good at filing things? Carla's hopeless when it comes to getting things in order.'

Janet felt a little overwhelmed. 'Where is Miss Ryder?' she asked, hesitantly.

'Mrs Ryder,' he corrected, with some emphasis. 'She insists on that.'

'I didn't know there was a Mr Ryder,' Janet said. Then, thinking of Ryder Hall, she added, 'He must be very — '

'I think, on the whole, Miss Lister, it would be better to take things as you find them,' Steve interrupted rather tartly. 'Carla doesn't take kindly to inquisitive people. On the other hand, let me tell you what you need to know. I'm Steve Trout. I'm Carla's agent, among other things. Usually there is a housekeeper, but Carla is thinking of selling the place again, and we're the only ones here at present.'

'I see,' Janet said, but she didn't.

'Carla has a villa on Spetse, and naturally, she has help there. You'll find life there a bit more organised. There's Elena and Georgios, Paul and — well, Carla will introduce you when you get there. In the meantime, I'll go and see if I can find you something to eat, even if it's only tea and biscuits. Carla should be down in a minute. I'll give her a call. You wait here.'

'Can I make a start on any of this?' Janet asked doubtfully.

'You're welcome to try,' Steve said cheerfully. 'Though it's no good asking me where anything goes. Only Carla can make any sense out of this stuff.'

When he was gone, she began to

collect the papers at random into loose bundles. She piled typewritten sheets on one side and anything handwritten on another. Suddenly a line of writing caught her eyes. She had seen it before. The same sentence leaped up at her, slightly amended, from the back of an envelope. She was looking at alternative drafts of the same paragraph.

Before she realised it, she was sorting the room. Within minutes she had reduced the drifts of paper on the floor into neat piles, ready for closer attention. She found a typewriter on the window-sill, buried under an avalanche of notes. She rescued it and turned her attention to the desk.

It was in a worse turmoil than the rest. Discarded sheets of papers were crumpled into little balls, and the desk was littered with half-finished pages and a welter of old pens and pencils. She began by ruthlessly consigning to the waste-bin both the screwed-up pages, and as many of the pens as no longer worked. The others she placed neatly together beside the blotting-pad.

As she did so, she became aware of something under the blotter. She took it out, expecting to find another card of notes, but this was not part of the manuscript.

It was a photograph. Quite an old photograph, by the look of it. A big, glossy, expensive photograph in a small, cardboard frame. From the picture there smiled a man, a man so devastatingly handsome that Janet could only gaze, fascinated. It was the man she had seen with Carla on television. A magnificent face. And across the photograph was written, in a bold, clear hand, 'For C, from P, with love.'

The corners of the photograph were frayed with time and use. Suddenly, there was a movement in the doorway, and a voice spoke.

'You can put that down.'

Janet dropped the photograph, and wheeled round. Carla Ryder stood in the doorway. She was wearing a very stylish, cream trouser-suit. The magnificent, red hair shone in a torrent over the neck and shoulders, and the beautiful face was distorted with anger.

'You can put that down,' she said again. 'The photograph,' she went on, as Janet stood there dumbly.

'Oh, the photograph,' Janet said, idiotically. She dropped it hurriedly on the desk.

'Not there.' Carla did not move from the door. 'Where you found it, underneath the blotter.'

Blushing, Janet replaced the picture.

'Now,' Carla said, fitting a cigarette into that famous holder, 'let me tell you one or two things. First, nobody touches my private belongings without my permission. Is that clear?'

'I'm very sorry,' Janet said humbly. 'I was only trying to tidy up.'

'Secondly,' Carla went on, as if Janet had not spoken, 'servants do not park their cars at the front of the house. And lastly, Miss Temporary

14

Secretary, or whoever you are, I do not employ young women who search my possessions while I am out of the room. So you can take yourself back to wherever you came from.' A gold lighter flared, and Carla took a deep puff on her cigarette. 'You're fired.'

'Can I come in?' It was Steve, edging his way around the door with a tray of tea and hot, buttered toast. 'I've brought you some breakfast.'

The sight and smell of the tray was almost the last straw. Janet's voice was distinctly wobbly as she said, with as much dignity as she could muster, 'Thank you, I shan't be needing it, Mr Trout. Mrs Ryder has decided that she doesn't require my services.'

Steve put the tray down on the corner of the desk.

'What brought that about? Seemed to me she might be ideal.'

Carla strode to the desk and took up the picture from under the blotter.

'Do you know what she was doing, Steve, when I came in? Searching my desk. I found her with this photograph in her hand.'

'I was trying to tidy up a bit,' Janet said. 'I moved the blotter and found the photograph. It was upside down. It just looked like a piece of card. If I'd realised it was private . . . ' She trailed off. 'Perhaps I shouldn't have done anything until Mrs Ryder gave me permission, but I thought that since you said I could — '

'You said she could move things?' Carla said to Steve, her voice sharp. 'That seems a bit stupid. Don't you think it would have been better to let me talk to the girl first? Besides, it's too late now. Nobody could possibly make sense of all this muddle except me. I've got different versions of some of the key scenes here, and now she has mixed them all up!'

'Actually, Mrs Ryder,' Janet put in gently, 'I tried to keep all the different versions together. I've got all the rewrites I could find over there on that chair.'

Carla looked at her for a moment in surprise, then went to the chair and riffled through the papers. When she spoke again there was a new quality in her voice. 'Well, you seem to have done quite a good job in a short time. I'll give you that.'

'And I,' Steve was saying, 'will give you this.' He handed Janet a cup of tea and a slice of toast. The scent of it made her mouth water. Nevertheless, she hesitated.

'Eat up,' Steve said. 'Now, listen, Carla. Obviously we can't have spying, but I did say that she could make a start. I'd no idea you'd a photograph of — that you had that photograph hidden away. Not very well hidden, either. Seems to me you ask for trouble.'

Carla's eyes flashed, but she said nothing. Janet took this as a good sign, and she sank her teeth into the toast. It was even better than it looked. She ate ravenously, scarcely hearing the conversation which passed between Carla and Steve. By the time she had finished, the atmosphere seemed distinctly more friendly.

'Well, all right,' Carla was saying, with a bad grace. 'If you think so. We'll give it a try for the next week. But I'm warning you, Steve, if anything goes wrong, I shall hold you personally responsible.'

'You need a secretary,' Steve said. 'You've got a week to get the book into something like a presentable form. Ye gods, is it any wonder I told the girl to get on with it.'

'OK, till Friday,' Carla said, but her eyes were still hostile as she turned to Janet. 'What's your name?'

'Lister. Janet Lister.'

'In the meantime, Miss Janet Lister, if you have quite finished eating toast, I would prefer it if you moved your car out of the front drive.'

Dumbly, Janet put down her cup and plate, stammered some thanks to Steve, and let herself out into the hall. She could not for a moment recall the way back to the front door, and as she stood

18

hesitating, she heard, unmistakably, the conversation from the study.

'Carla, darling,' Steve was saying. 'Was that really necessary?'

'Steve, I saw her with the photograph. What was I supposed to think? I wish I didn't need a secretary just now, but with two deadlines coming up — '

'Anyway,' Steve said, 'the more ordinary life looks to the casual observer, the better. That's why I think you ought to take her to Spetse. In any case, the whole business will soon be over. You'll just have to be more careful.'

'I suppose so,' Carla said. 'I'm just sorry it had to start out like this.'

Steve laughed. 'Yes, I can see why it gave you a nasty turn, but I'm sure it was purely innocent. And she seems ideal in every other way. Look how she's transformed this study.'

'Yes,' Carla said grudgingly. 'She seems willing.'

'She seems very nice,' Steve said. 'And you'd better be pleasant to her if you want to keep her. The way you're acting you're bound to arouse suspicions. She must already know there's something odd about that photograph.'

Carla laughed. 'Oh, she'll do, I dare say. I told the agency I wanted someone fairly unattractive, and she's certainly that! We can't afford to have all the young men from the island buzzing about like bees again. That hair! And those clothes! You know, Steve, the poor little thing is positively plain.'

Outside in her car, the positively plain, little thing found that her vision was misted by something that was not rain.

★ ★ ★

The next few days passed in a haze. Janet worked steadily, and gradually she saw the typescript of the novel begin to emerge. Carla sat for hours working with her at the desk. The photograph, however, had vanished.

20

There were interruptions, too. Journalists, and, every mealtime, it seemed, a different, young man in an expensive car would come for Carla. For each, Carla had a different, elegant outfit, and the same radiant, special smile.

Only Steve was there to share Janet's snatched meals. He was always courteous, but whenever Carla left the house, he seemed distracted.

She saw them together on Wednesday evening, in the hall. That evening's handsome, young man was at the door and Carla was stunning in a green evening dress. Steve was helping with her wrap, when suddenly he pulled Carla to him and kissed her hair.

'Never mind,' he whispered soothingly, 'it won't be for ever.'

Janet was embarrassed and at a loss. For the second time, she appeared to be spying. She turned round, shutting the study door with a sharp bang. The two figures in the hall sprung apart instantly. Janet walked towards them.

21

'Just finished?' Carla asked, more warmly than usual.

'Yes,' Janet replied, as casually as she could.

'You'd better get packed then,' Carla said. 'We're leaving tomorrow.'

A look passed between her and Steve. Janet wondered what it meant. She had already noticed that there was real affection between Steve and Carla. The way they talked to one another, the familiar way he dropped his arm on to her shoulder, that kiss. They shared a house, after all, and it was Steve, always, who waited up for Carla's return, long after Janet had gone to bed. But why, then, the succession of handsome, young men? And where was Mr Ryder? Janet felt very young, and very naïve.

She went up to her room to pack her possessions — her clothes were not exactly suitable for Greece. There was her grey coat, plus two or three working suits, some sensible skirts and a couple of sundresses bought for her

22

holiday in Majorca. When Carla paid her, she vowed, she would splash out. On this salary, she could afford it.

The telephone rang. Janet went reluctantly down to the study and lifted the receiver. 'Ryder Hall,' she said. 'Mrs Ryder's secretary speaking.'

There was a long silence. Then a male voice, educated and slightly foreign, said, 'Is Carla there?'

'I'm afraid not,' Janet said politely. 'Perhaps I could take a message?'

Another silence. 'I really need to speak to Mrs Ryder,' the voice said at last.

'I don't know what time she'll be back,' Janet said, 'and we're leaving for the airport first thing in the morning. Mrs Ryder is going to Greece.'

'I know.' The voice was rather sharp.

'I could give her a message,' Janet said, 'if it's urgent.'

'Oh, yes. It's urgent.' The voice seemed to hesitate, and then went on, 'Tell her it's off. Tell her it will have to be postponed.'

'Postponed,' Janet echoed foolishly. 'What will have to be postponed?'

'That's all. Just tell her the whole operation will have to be postponed. Say I'm sorry not to have spoken to her personally, but I can't get the team together that I was hoping for. Have you got that?'

'Whom shall I say called?' Janet was taking shorthand furiously.

The voice laughed shortly. 'She'll know.'

As soon as Carla returned, Janet delivered the message. The effect was startling. Carla turned pale, clutching at her chair. Steve was at her side at once.

'I think,' Steve said, gently, 'that Carla would appreciate a cup of tea.'

Janet knew that she was being dismissed, and she went to make the tea. She took her time, realising that Steve and Carla wanted time to talk.

On her way back, she met Steve, and, taking her courage into both hands, she asked him outright what the call meant.

'It's about the book,' Steve said, but he did not meet her eyes, and Janet knew he was lying. He went past her up the stairs, his face clouded.

In the study, Carla was asleep, her head on her arm. She had been crying. On the floor, fallen from the limp hand, was the photograph.

Janet bent and picked it up, just as Steve came into the study. At once she was on the defensive. 'Mrs Ryder dropped this,' she said gently.

Steve nodded. 'You don't know that face?' he said.

'I think I saw it once, on television,' Janet said, and then more boldly, 'Who is it?'

'Well, you're going to Spetse,' Steve said. 'You might as well know. His name is Stavropolous. Does that mean anything to you?'

'Steve!' Carla Ryder had snapped awake. 'That's enough!'

'But if you're taking her to Spetse.'

'I am not taking her to Spetse,' Carla said. She sounded reckless. 'That telephone call has changed everything. I shall have to stay in England for a fortnight to make other arrangements. Janet can go on to Spetse alone.'

'Alone?' Janet's voice was a croak.

'Carla, you can't,' Steve said again.

'Why not? Everything is already arranged. Paul is coming to the airport and Elena will have prepared food for the week-end. There's the film version of 'Love Among the Lilacs' to type. It's scattered all over my study at the villa.'

Steve opened his mouth to speak, but no sound came. It was Janet who said, 'How shall I know where to go and everything?' This sudden change of plan had set her heart thumping.

'Oh, Steve and I will take you to the airport, won't we, Steve?'

'You'll never get away with it,' Steve said, as if to himself. Carla ignored him.

'And Paul will meet the aeroplane at the other end and take you to the villa.'

'And how will I recognise Paul?' Janet asked numbly.

Carla laughed. It was not a pleasant laugh. There was a certain bitter edge to it. 'Oh, you'll know Paul,' she said. 'You could hardly miss him. He looks remarkably like that photograph you're holding.'

'Carla.' Steve's voice was full of warning.

'What is it, Steve?' Carla said in a voice that was so brittle it was near to breaking. 'There's only one face in the world that looks anything like that photograph. Isn't that true?'

Steve turned away.

'Well, then,' Carla went on, 'that's settled. I'd have an early night if I were you. You'll have a busy day tomorrow.'

And with that, Janet had to be content.

# 2

The day that followed was certainly busy. Afterwards, Janet found she could scarcely remember a single feature of the journey, until she found herself accompanied by her two cases on a trolley, in the terminal building at Athens.

She stood a moment blinking in the afternoon sunlight. Her passport bore a stamp in letters she did not understand, and all around her was a hubbub of unfamiliar language. She had no Greek currency and very little English money, and she spoke no word of the language. What would happen to her if the famous Paul did not arrive to claim her?

Hesitantly, she edged towards a desk, and tried to pluck up the courage to speak to the girl behind the desk.

Suddenly, the girl said, smiling,

'Can I help you?'

'Oh, you speak English? Someone was supposed to meet me, and I was a bit worried because I don't speak any Greek.'

'You need not be alarmed,' the girl said. 'Most employees of the airport speak English. I advise you to seek your friend at the information desk.'

Janet looked in the direction she was indicating. There was a large desk, and above it, in clear English, a notice said, Information and Enquiries.

Cheeks blazing, she joined the short queue at the desk. A tall man at the head of the queue was talking to the information clerk, in Greek. A new panic seized her. Was this Paul Stavropolous? He must be Greek himself. What if he couldn't speak English?

The information clerk repeated 'Stavropolous,' and then, 'Janet Lister.' He moved towards the loudspeaker microphone.

The tall man half-turned his head,

and Janet glimpsed his face for the first time. With the same dark eyes and the same smile, he was a little less handsome, perhaps, than the photograph suggested.

The man was speaking again, in Greek, and Janet's heart sank. There was nothing for it. She took a deep breath and stepped forward. She spoke deliberately loudly and clearly. 'Me Janet Lister. You Mr Stavropolous?'

He looked at her, at first in surprise, and then with dawning amusement. His dark eyes held hers. 'Yes,' he said at last, 'me Mr Stavropolous. How do you do, Janet Lister? I can see that Carla has given you her usual clear picture of exactly what to expect. I hope you had a good journey. Welcome to Greece.'

Janet could feel the blush flooding her face. How could she have been so foolish? She did not know how to look at him, or how to speak to him again. She bit her lip, and a tear trembled on her cheek.

He noticed, and suddenly he smiled, with a warmth which almost tipped her outright into tears.

'All the best people talk this way,' he said. 'It's been the start of some wonderful friendships. Me Tarzan, you Janet. Come on, Janet. Are these your suitcases?' And taking one in each hand, he led the way to the waiting car.

The drive down the peninsula was delightful. There were signs in the unfamiliar alphabet, little villages which clustered up hillsides. Once, even, she saw an old woman sitting in the fading light, spinning, and at her feet a young man sitting playing a bazouki. Olive trees stumbled out of an arid landscape, and at last, as the daylight faded, the dark mass of the great hills took shape.

And always, there was the dark, disturbing presence of the young man at her side. Paul drove with careless ease, negotiating steep curves and winding streets with nonchalant skill. He talked little, but allowed her to lapse into silence, as the brilliant golden afternoon waned into sudden, dark-blue night.

'You speak very good English,' Janet ventured at last.

He smiled. 'I ought to,' he said. 'I have special advantages. My mother was English.'

'But you speak Greek, too. I heard you,' Janet exclaimed.

He grinned. 'Then again,' he said, 'my father was Greek.'

'Oh, how silly of me,' Janet said in genuine confusion. 'It's been a confusing day — the aeroplane — first class, too. All those foreigners. Oh, dear, I didn't mean you —'

He laughed again, and she found herself talking, too much perhaps, telling him all about herself, her mother, the trip to Majorca.

'That must have been nice,' he said encouragingly.

She sighed. 'I suppose it was. I was pretty miserable at that time.'

He shot her a glance. 'A man?'

She nodded. 'A man. I'm over it now, I think.'

There was a long, long silence. 'It can take a long time,' he said. And then, almost as if he wished to change the subject, 'There you are, Janet, the sea.'

It was so beautiful, with the silver light dancing on the rippling waters, that it was moments before Janet found her voice.

'It's wonderful,' she breathed.

'Appearances can be deceptive,' Paul said sombrely.

'What do you mean?' she said, alarmed by his tone.

'Oh,' he said, more lightly, 'the sea has moods, like people.'

Janet looked at him dumbly, uncertain what to think.

He opened the car door. 'Come on, Janet, time to go to the boat.'

'The boat?'

He laughed. 'How would you get to an island?' he asked smiling. 'Would you prefer to swim?'

A large motor-launch bobbed gently at a little jetty.

'Georgios, wake up,' Paul shouted. The cabin door opened and Janet was helped aboard.

She had never been on a private boat before, and her feelings were a mixture of apprehension and wonder. Wonder at the comfort and size of the large cabin and the luxury of the fitments and anxiety as the boat rose and fell beneath her feet. Instinctively, she reached out her hand. He took it and gave it a reassuring squeeze.

'I don't feel very safe,' she whispered. 'Boats worry me.'

His reply surprised her. 'It's all right, Janet. I feel that way myself, sometimes.'

'You?' She found it hard to believe. 'But you were bred on the island. You must have spent your life around boats.'

He squeezed her hand again. 'There was a time — ' He stopped. 'But these days I rely on Georgios.' He nodded towards the man who had answered his shout. 'Miss Lister, Georgios. We couldn't manage without him.'

Georgios laughed, showing white teeth. 'Mr Paul is right,' he said, with a wild wave of his hand. 'Without me — nothing. You sit down now. Ten minutes, maybe fifteen. I take you to Spetse.'

He disappeared into the wheelhouse, and soon there was a gentle rumble from the engine. Georgios slipped the rope from the mooring and the boat crept out to sea. Janet strained to catch a view from the large landscape window.

'Paul,' she said presently, 'I'd love to go on deck. You wouldn't — I mean, would you — please, will you come with me?'

A spasm of some emotion crossed his face, but he stood up at once, and held out his hand to her. 'Come on then,' he said.

They went together into the silver night. Janet trembled a little in the night breeze. At once, Paul took off his coat and slipped it over her shoulders.

'It's chilly,' he said. His arm was around her waist, and he did not move it, but held her as though to restrain and guard her. She was strangely, actively aware of his dark, handsome presence.

Neither of them spoke nor moved again until the boat edged into a long sloping bay, and the engines died. Georgios was ashore, manhandling the luggage almost before the boat had stopped.

Suddenly, the foreshore was flooded with light. Ahead, on the side of the hill, lay a huge, rambling villa and even by the light of the lamps, Janet could see the flowering vines which covered the walls, and the outline of a long, low veranda. On the other side of the landing stage a huge yacht lay at anchor.

'Is that yours?' she said to Paul. 'Do you sail that?'

'There was a time — ' he said softly.

Somewhere in the darkness a door was flung open, and the faint scent of flowers was joined by a new aroma — the unmistakable savour of roast lamb.

'Come along, Janet,' Paul said, as Georgios set off up the sloping path with a suitcase in each hand. 'We've arrived.'

Dinner was delicious. Elena, who proved to be very young and very pretty, not only cooked the meal, but also waited at table. She was attentive to Janet and obviously devoted to Paul. He was so naturally at home in the villa that it came as a bolt from the blue to Janet when he suddenly rose to his feet.

'Well,' he said, 'I must say goodnight.' He moved to the french windows, which led from the dining-room on to the long veranda.

'But don't you live in the villa?' Once the words were out, Janet could have bitten her tongue. Why should she have supposed such a thing? But there had been something about his manner, as if he owned the place.

He shook his head at her, and the dark eyes, humorous but deep, held hers for a long moment. 'In the villa, yes, in a manner of speaking. But — well — let's just say I have my own apartments. And now, Janet, you are tired. It has been a long day for you. Elena will show you to your room. Sleep well.' And he was gone, and in passing his hand brushed her shoulder.

She sat for long minutes at the empty table, gazing at the place where he had been. She had known him for less than half a day, and already he dominated her thoughts.

She pulled herself together with an effort, and found Elena staring at her. She smiled, rather wanly at the girl.

'That was an excellent meal, Elena,' she said. 'Delicious.'

The girl beamed. She was really extremely attractive, Janet thought. Carla seemed to surround herself with beautiful people. Elena, Steve, Paul — here Janet's heart gave an uncontrollable lurch. Only she, herself, was the exception to the rule. 'Plain' Carla had called her.

'You liked?' Elena was clearly delighted to be praised. 'I make again for you this lamb. It's special Greek recipe. Come now, and I will show to you your room.' She led the way upstairs.

It was beautiful. There was no other word for it. After her little bedsit in London it was like a mansion. There was a private bathroom, an easy chair, her own balcony overlooking the patio and the sea. She exclaimed in delight at it.

'Oh, it's lovely, lovely.'

Elena shrugged. 'Is very nice. Now is my weekend. Do you need somethings? Soon my brother comes and I must to go to my house, so what you needing you asking quickly.'

'No, no,' Janet said. 'You go along now. I'll have a bath and go to bed.'

'Is plenty water tonight,' Elena said mysteriously. Only later did Janet learn that Spetse's water arrived by tanker, and supplies were sometimes limited. Tonight, however, she knew nothing of this, and she went into the bathroom blithely, and ran herself a bath. Elena was right, there was plenty water, and it was plenty hot! Elena was still lingering at the door.

'Nothings you want? Mr Stavropolous, Paul, said I was to see you have everythings you want.'

'Yes, Elena, really,' Janet insisted. 'I have everythings what I want.'

Janet lay in the perfumed water longer than she should have, thinking about how thoughtful Paul was being. She was already beginning to feel that it was typical of the man. The small kindnesses he had shown her were proof of that. Paul Stavropolous was certainly an unusual man.

She went to bed with her heart singing. Somewhere deep down, her old caution stirred. 'Too good to be true.' She closed her eyes and tried to take a grip on reality by recalling David Cambay, but it was no good. The face which came to her mind was dark and powerful, with deep, brown eyes and lips which smiled and called her Janet . . .

She woke, the next morning, to brilliant sunshine, and a hasty glance at the bedroom clock told her that it was ten-thirty. She tumbled out of bed, had a hasty wash, slipped into a sundress and made her way to the dining-room.

Everything was in apple-pie order, polished, swept and cleaned, but there was no sign of breakfast. Janet called, several times, but only the sunshine answered her, streaming in at the door as she opened it.

Even then it was some minutes before realisation dawned. Of course, she had been warned. Elena had the weekend off. Last night she should have been asking intelligent questions about where to find everything. Well, she would have to explore, do something, if she was to eat before Monday.

The kitchen was next door to the dining-room. It was modern and well stocked. Eggs, fruit, vegetables, milk and bread were ranged within easy reach, and also something which Janet had not been prepared for, a crate of bottled drinking water.

She found some coffee, and, lacking a kettle, boiled some water in a saucepan. A piece of the fresh bread and some butter completed her makeshift breakfast, which she ate looking down towards the harbour.

She noticed that the landing-stage was empty. No Paul. Her heart sank. She tidied away the plate and cup and set off to find Carla's study. If she couldn't find Paul, she could at least work, but the study was difficult to find. Besides the dining-room, there appeared to be three or four large sitting-rooms, all with breathtaking views. There were two bathrooms, a sauna, a huge laundry room, but still no study.

A little embarrassed, Janet turned back to the other wing of the villa. Carla had clearly said that there was a study. She felt ill-at-ease as she tried the doors, one after another. Several bedrooms were clearly used as guest rooms; another, full of dresses and shoes topsy-turvy on the bed — Elena's room, obviously. Janet shut the door quickly.

She walked down a narrow passage. A gold and white door led into a dressing-room; and a big master bedroom. Carla's, naturally. Everything was covered in blue satin, the walls were mirrored, and in the centre, on a deep, white, wall-to-wall rug, was a huge, heart-shaped bed.

On the far side of the room there was another door, through which Janet could see a luxury bathroom with tiled floors and a huge, sunken bath.

Next to the bathroom, another door, gold and white like the first. Not the study, surely? Not even Carla would have a study leading directly off her bedroom, would she?

Feeling like a burglar, Janet tiptoed across the room and turned the handle. It didn't budge. There was no key, but the door was locked. A cupboard, perhaps?

Guiltily, she stepped back into the hall, and tried the only remaining door, across the passage from her own bedroom. A familiar jumble of papers, books and manuscripts met her eyes. This was unmistakably the study. Carla had been right — there was plenty to do.

It was several hours before she looked up from her sorting, and headed back to the kitchen for cheese, fruit and coffee. Once more she sat at the window, gazing out at the brilliant blue of the sky and sea. As she watched, she became aware of two things — first, a white dot out there on the water, and second, from the window she could see that the villa had a second wing, a whole section stretching out down to the sea.

'Separate apartments,' Paul had said. Yet into that other section there could be no other entry from the villa than the door in Carla's bedroom . . .

The white shape on the water took on a recognisable form. It was the yacht which Janet had seen the night before. Transfixed, she watched as the boat turned into the wind, the sails tumbled, and the great, white hull edged gently up to the quay. A slim, tall figure, dressed in dazzling white, leaped lightly over the side and made fast. Janet looked for the stalwart form of Georgios, but there was no sign of him.

Paul bundled the sail up loosely, and came up the path, whistling. Janet's eyes were fixed on him, helplessly. Surely he had said last night that he didn't sail anymore? He didn't look like a man who was nervous of the sea. On the contrary, he seemed very pleased with himself as he strode up the path, and disappeared around the far wing of the villa.

Janet rose guiltily, swept up the crumbs from the table, and tied her hair hastily into a plait, and waited.

Paul didn't come.

Janet waited for half an hour before she stepped out into the sunshine, and down the zig-zag path towards the sea. As she walked past the corner of the villa, she found another door opening on to the path. Paul had gone into the other wing of the villa.

She stepped forward, gazing at the door. It was half-concealed by creeper, almost as if it was meant to be hidden. Certainly she had not noticed it the night before. She swallowed hard. Was there a movement behind the curtain? She raised her hand to knock on the door.

A hand closed over hers.

'No need, Janet. Were you looking for me?' Paul was behind her, still dazzling in his sailing whites. His face was smiling, but she could sense the tension behind it.

'You came up the path and then disappeared.' Janet faltered. 'I didn't know where — '

The tension vanished, and the magnificent eyes and lips were smiling with a kindness which put her instantly at ease.

'I see. Well, there is no mystery, Janet. I told you, I had my own apartments. Here they are, my humble abode. I often eat in the main villa, but I have my own rooms, an office and a kitchen, too, come to that. So I hadn't fallen from the face of the earth, little Janet, just gone home to roost.'

Janet managed a smile. 'I didn't mean to pry.'

'Pry?' His grin was infectious. 'Of course you didn't. Mysteries are made to be cleared up. And while you are in an exploring mood, would you like to look over my island later on?'

'In the car?' Janet stammered.

Paul shook his head. 'There aren't many cars on Spetse,' he said. 'There's

47

a motor-bike, if you can ride it, but Georgios usually takes us over to the town in the launch. Or we walk if we feel enterprising. It's not all that far, but it's pretty steep, and it can be very hot. It's not too bad at this time of year.'

'I feel enterprising,' Janet said firmly, rather to her own surprise.

'Very well,' he agreed. 'A walk it shall be. Make sure you're wearing comfortable shoes. I tell you what, Janet. Tarzan will take you over his kingdom later in the afternoon. And then we will eat in one of the tavernas in Spetse town tonight. Would you like that?'

Janet was too delighted to do more than nod, her eyes shining.

'That's settled then. And now, what would you like to do while we are waiting? Swim? Sit on the patio?'

Janet muttered something about having work to do, and escaped into the study with burning cheeks, and a thumping heart.

She settled down among the fragments of Carla's prose and began to work, but her mind would not behave. Every heroine in every scene was Janet herself, every embrace was with Paul, every moonlight rendezvous a promise for her own evening.

And yet, wasn't this the man whose photograph graced Carla's desk? And she was going to dinner with him. David, her mind warned her, remember David.

And then she answered herself. Remember Carla. All those young men. Carla standing in Steve's arms. What could she care for this handsome, young man thousands of miles across the sea? Yet this was the man with whom Carla shared her home. And, she realised with a little shock, he could only have come up behind her today by coming through the locked door into Carla's bedroom.

One of the telephones shrilled — an unfamiliar tone to Janet's English ear, but she picked it up, and answered

49

it. A voice spoke in Greek, and then Carla's voice. 'Janet? You arrived all right? Have you started on the manuscript yet?'

Janet began to answer, but Carla cut her short. 'Yes, well, never mind all that. Have a go at it when you have a moment. Oh, and on Monday, tell Elena to get some chicken. She'll produce that wretched lamb of hers every day if you let her. Not that Paul would complain, but it isn't everybody's favourite. How is Paul by the way? Taking care of you? I told him to take you to a taverna tonight.' A few more instructions, and then she was gone.

'I told him to take you to a taverna.' The words echoed in Janet's mind. She looked at herself in the mirror. Her hair was bedraggled, her nose red from the sun, and the sundress seemed somehow terribly unflattering.

By the time Paul came to call for her, reddened eyes had made the situation even worse.

The sunshine and the vivid green

of the olive groves revived her, and Paul walked beside her up the long, stony slope. It was steep and Janet was beginning to feel very tired and hot.

She could feel her hair escaping from the plait which secured it, her face glowed with exertion, and her shoulders were turning pink from the sun. She must look a sight, she thought wearily.

'Look behind you,' Paul said. 'It's worth the climb.'

Janet looked. It was a little piece of heaven. The white boat, the villa with its frame of blossoms, the green leaves, the sapphire sea.

'It's lovely,' she said. And they stood for a moment, drinking it in. Then Paul led the way into the cool, welcoming wood.

The trees were not thick, but they were high and smelled of pine and sunshine, and the path beneath them, although steep, was shady.

A lock of hair escaped and fell across her face. She tried to push it back, fumbled, failed, and impatiently released her hair and began separating it once more to tie it up again. Paul was beside her in an instant.

'No, Janet,' he said, restraining her hand. 'Don't.' His hand raised her hair gently and resettled it deftly around her shoulders. 'That's better. Such pretty hair. Why do you tie it back in that ridiculous way?'

Janet looked at him. She was aware of her unflattering sundress, of her pink nose and her dusty feet. 'Do you think it's ridiculous?' she asked tremulously. 'It's supposed to make me look efficient. Like the glasses. I look childish without them.' Her voice broke. 'Carla said I was positively plain. And you think I look ridiculous.' It was no good pretending. Two hot tears coursed down her face.

Paul looked at her with sudden concern, and she saw in his eyes something more than politeness. It was as if he saw her for the first time. 'Poor, little Janet,' he said gently. 'Let me see.' He took the heavy glasses from her nose, and lifted her face to his. 'Do you need these?'

Janet shook her head. 'No,' she said humbly.

'Foolish Janet,' Paul said quietly, gazing down into her eyes.

Somehow she didn't feel foolish any more. His hand rearranged her hair, lifting it forward, framing her face.

'No,' he said at last, as if he had given the matter a lot of serious thought. 'Not childish.' His fingers swept over her cheek, smoothing the place where the tears had been. 'High cheekbones, lovely skin, beautiful eyes. No, Janet. You're certainly not plain. Young perhaps, and vulnerable. So vulnerable that it almost seems a crime to do this.' His mouth bent to hers, and the next moment she was crushed into his arms. She sank into sweetness, and the next moment he released her.

She raised her eyes to his, and felt the colour mount to her cheeks. 'You look lovely when you blush,' Paul said, with a return to the old, mocking style. 'Don't blush any more, or I'll do it again.'

He didn't, though, and they walked the rest of the way in silence, and Janet could feel her cheeks burning, all the way into Spetse town.

# 3

Spetse town entranced her from the first. The narrow, winding lanes, the churches with their whitewashed bell-towers, the black-hatted priests, the shops tumbling on to the pavements.

When a horse-drawn taxi clopped lazily into view, she was bewitched. Paul hailed it, and it bore them down the twisting streets on to the square, where men and women sat, drinking coffee or aperitifs in the slanting sunlight.

The rest of the evening passed in a dream. They had coffee at a street café, watching the boats come and go across the rippling tide, and a laughter-filled shopping expedition. Paul dragged Janet into a little shop.

'Buy yourself a dress,' he urged. 'A new dress, for the Janet who lets her hair down and doesn't wear glasses.'

'I haven't any money,' Janet faltered. 'That is, I haven't been paid yet.'

'Well, see what you like, anyway,' Paul pressed.

Janet moved through the dresses, and hesitantly picked one.

'Oh, no, my Janet,' Paul protested. 'This is for you.' He took from the rack a simple dress in white cotton, with a narrow, printed border and square-cut neckline.

Janet couldn't imagine herself in such a dress. Paul spoke a few words to the Greek woman who was hovering hopefully at the door. 'You can try it on.'

Janet slipped behind the curtain, smoothed the white folds into place and buckled on the heavy belt Paul handed her.

'There's a mirror out here,' he called, and Janet came out.

What she saw astonished her. Gone was the skinny girl with the severe hairstyle and the narrow face. From the mirror there smiled a woman whose shining hair swung about slim shoulders and whose dress emphasised her girlish figure. Here was a woman whose eyes shone, and whose lips were half-parted in a delighted smile.

'We'll take it,' Paul said, and then softly to Janet. 'A present. A thank you for the kiss.'

'I shouldn't take it,' Janet protested.

'Neither should I,' Paul said gently. 'But I did. So this is thank you and then we're quits.'

They ate in a taverna, and Janet discovered more Greek food. She had never eaten moussaka, and she loved it. Paul, however, ate something which he could not persuade her to sample.

'Octopus?' she repeated, horrified.

'Octopus!' he replied, and much later, after the wine, and the coffee, and the Greek dancing, he took her to the waterfront, and showed her the octopus hung up to dry, and the little boats which were, even now, bringing in their catch across the moonlit bay.

And, at last, one of the little boats

was Georgios, and they stood on the deck, hand in hand, watching the wake creaming across the sea.

He did not kiss her again when they parted but, in the long mirror in her room, Janet glimpsed again the slim, happy young woman in the dazzling, simple, white dress. Her face was alight with the memory of that kiss, her cheeks aflame and her eyes afire.

No, the reflection told her she was certainly not plain.

The next day she did not see Paul all morning. Once she thought she heard him moving about the villa. She washed her hair, and brushed till it shone. She slipped on the new dress, and hovered in the sitting-room, sipping coffee. Paul did not come.

After lunch — Janet ate too much because she was miserable — she went back into the study and forgot her unhappiness, as she had learned to do in the past, by losing herself in her work. Finally, with a heavy heart, she went to her room and hung the crisp, white dress back on its hanger.

The afternoon dragged dismally, and it seemed as if the weather caught her mood. The blue sky clouded into angry grey; a sudden gust of wind rattled the windows, and within half an hour it was raining, great, heavy drops, that seemed as if the sky itself was weeping.

Janet pulled the curtains and closed the shutters. She spread out the piles of paper that would become Carla Ryder's new movie. She rolled the paper into the machine and began to type, numbing herself with it, until the rain stopped, and the light began to fade. Only then did she go back to the kitchen. She was too dispirited to cook anything, so she took a plate of fruit, poured herself a coffee, and wandered out on to the patio to watch the sun drown in the ripples, and the stars emerge softly into the velvet night.

She sat for a long time and the noises of the night rose around her. The whirring of beetles, the plop of a fish, the rattle of cicadas.

And then, somewhere closer at hand, another sound. A rustle, a footstep? Then, unmistakably, on to the scented air, the odour of tobacco wafting up, drowning the scent of blossom, and the sweet smell of the sea.

Janet raised her head sharply. At once she felt the darkness stiffen, as if it, too, was listening. She strained her eyes, but she could see nothing.

'Paul,' she called. Carefully, she set her plate down on the white gleam that was the table, and walked, uncertainly in the darkness, towards the corner of the villa. That, surely, was where the smoke was coming from.

'Paul?' she called again. Nothing but the night answered her. She peered again, desperately, into the waiting, watching darkness. Did she imagine it or was there a figure there, a glimmer in the shadows? 'Paul?'

The glimmer in the shadows was moving slowly, so slowly it was difficult to detect, sliding into the darkness, and around the corner of the villa, back down the path towards the sea.

'Paul?' Janet's cry was despairing. For a long time there was silence, and then faint and distant, but unmistakable, the sound of a door being quietly, but firmly closed.

Monday morning brought Elena, singing enthusiastically in the kitchen, but there was no sign of Paul as Janet breakfasted on fresh rolls and luscious fruit.

' 'Morning, Elena. Hello, Janet. I must have smelled the coffee.' And there was Paul, relaxed and smiling, framed in the golden sunlight of the door.

He smiled at her, with evident pleasure.

'Elena, that coffee smells heavenly. I know I've had breakfast, but I can't resist it. I'll have some more.' His hand ruffled Janet's hair. 'And where is your white dress, young lady?' He was sitting beside her, dark eyes laughing with an ease which was reassuring.

'I wore it for a while yesterday,' Janet said coolly.

'I'm sorry I missed it then,' Paul said lightly, with one of his brilliant smiles. 'I was away all day yesterday. I hoped to get back in the evening, and perhaps we could have had supper on the balcony. I could have shown you where the dolphins leap.' The eyes which smiled into hers were as deep and untroubled as ever.

She bit her lip. 'I thought I saw you,' she blurted out. 'After it got dark, over on the balcony path, down by your door. I called, but you didn't answer.'

There was a sudden, still silence. Paul and Elena both stiffened, noticeably, and Janet could have sworn that a glance passed between them, sharp, secret and meaningful. Then Paul laughed. Not an easy laugh, but it broke the tension.

'Oh,' he said, smiling, as he handed his cup to her for another refill. 'It must have been Georgios.'

Of course. Janet flamed at the cheeks. Georgios. Why hadn't she thought of that. 'Why did he slink off like that?' she wondered aloud.

'If you knew Georgios, you would be glad he did slink away,' Paul said, with a kind of determined jollity.

Elena laughed, rather a nervous laugh, and the hand that poured the coffee trembled slightly. Was Janet imagining it, or was there an air of relief?

Paul chattered on, praising Elena for the coffee, complimenting Janet on her dedication to work the day before. 'Although I'm sorry about the dress,' he said. 'It completes the transformation.' He leaned forward, and lifted a lock of her hair with one finger. 'You know, Janet, you waste yourself. You're a lovely, lovely woman. You have beautiful hair, a sweet face and a pretty figure. I want to bring out more of the real you. It's like watching a bud blossom into a flower.'

Janet's eyes shone. Not even David

had ever told her she was beautiful. She glimpsed her reflection in the long mirror. At that instant she knew she was beautiful, but in that mirror, she saw something else. Something which disturbed her, and took her sparkle from her face. Reflected in the glass, she saw Elena, still with the coffee pot in her hand, frozen into a position which was rigid with displeasure. Janet stared in amazement.

Paul's glance followed her own, and he turned to Elena sharply. She reddened, and, collecting plates and cups from the table, said something in Greek. Paul answered her, not harshly, but with vigour, and Elena burst forth into a torrent of words, eyes flashing.

Paul looked at her for a moment, and then said something very quietly, very gently. Elena stopped, and setting down the dishes on the table, rushed from the room. From the kitchen, Janet could hear the sound of quiet sobbing.

Paul excused himself, and followed

her. Janet buttered herself another roll she didn't really want to cover her embarrassment. Elena couldn't be jealous, could she? Paul treated Elena like one of the family, but there was no hint of any deeper relationship. And yet — there was something.

Paul came back, smiling ruefully. 'I'm sorry about that,' he said, with real apology. 'There are, well, one or two problems in the family. Nothing that need affect you. Truly. I'm sorry.'

He came over and took her hands, raising her to her feet. At that moment, Elena came in with a tray.

Janet expected another heated outburst, but Elena merely glanced at Paul with a kind of despairing dignity, and said to Janet, 'I sorry, Miss Janet. I bit upset. Is my sister, she die not long ago.' She threw Paul a searing look, as if there was some other meaning in the words.

'It's over now, Elena,' Paul said almost tenderly. 'It's time to forget it.'

Elena nodded, speechless, and began to gather the things from the table. Janet caught a glimpse of eyes which brimmed with tears, and when Elena had gone back to the kitchen, she turned to Paul.

'Is she all right?' she whispered.

'Yes, she's fine,' Paul said. 'You heard what she said. It's the simple truth. She's upset about her sister. Honestly.' He turned her face to his, and kissed her gently on the lips. 'Trust me?'

If only I could, Janet thought to herself, even as her lips parted hungrily against his. If only I could. For something else had come into her consciousness.

Last night, on the patio, she had noticed particularly that there was no sign of the motor-boat, or of the yacht. Therefore, Georgios hadn't been there.

Janet said nothing.

Paul's lips sought hers for an instant, and then he released her, a kiss brushing her ear.

'I could stay here all day with you, Janet,' he said, the brilliant smile lighting his eyes. 'But duty calls. I shall see you at dinner, perhaps.' And he was gone.

Janet returned to the study, and worked until Elena called her to lunch. It seemed a lonely meal, and even Elena showed no inclination to talk.

'If you want, Miss Janet,' she said shyly, at the end of the meal, 'I can bring you somethings in the study when you working. Then you don't have for sitting out here on your owns. You like?'

Janet smiled and nodded.

'Or outside in the sun shinings,' Elena went on. 'Is nice outside for eating.'

And so it was decided. If Paul was not there for lunch, Janet would eat hers in the study or on the terrace. She went back to work and stilled her fluttering heart with more typing. At three, Elena appeared, as if by magic, with a pitcher of iced fruit juice. Janet drank it gratefully.

'Why you not go for swimming?' Elena said. 'Is a hot day. Miss Carla, she always go for swimming in the afternoon. Sometimes even in the night.'

The idea, once put to her, seemed irresistible. Janet went out on to the terrace, and looked at the deep, unbroken blue of the sea. There was no beach, but there were steps on the edge of the jetty. She slipped back into her room, and changed into a swimming costume, draped a towel across her shoulders, and came out once more on to the terrace.

She took off her watch and sunglasses and ran down to the sea. The water was colder than it looked, but after a moment, Janet caught her breath. She gazed up at the shore, at the pink and white of the villa set in the green and gold of the hillside, at where she and Paul had walked, at her own bedroom, with its balcony overlooking the patio. A fortnight ago she had been in London, jobless, in the rain. So much had happened so quickly.

She turned over in the clear water, and began to swim, round the edge of the little bay, into a sheltered cove. It was entirely deserted, with only a handful of olive trees dappling down to the water. There were big, flat rocks close to the water's edge. She swam in and began to walk ashore, but the sharpness of the stones hurt her feet, and she turned back into deeper water. At a different stage of the tide, perhaps, you could swim in, right up to those rocks, and have a private beach all to yourself. Another day.

Something brushed her hand, and she looked down at it surprised. Jellyfish! Huge, white blobs floating in on the lapping waves. In fact, once you had seen them, they seemed to be everywhere.

Struggling with panic, Janet struck out for the jetty again. Jellyfish seemed to bar her way, but at last she had climbed the steps, and reclaimed her towel, without being stung. She ran all the way back to the villa.

Elena had come out on the terrace to watch her come. 'Miss Janet, are you all right. Have somethings ate you?'

In spite of herself, Janet smiled, and began to towel her streaming hair. She explained about the jellyfish.

Elena listened gravely. 'Was they white or reds?' she asked when Janet had finished.

'White,' Janet said. 'Enormous.' She made a shape in her hands.

'Is all right,' Elena said, smiling in relief. 'White ones they no bite you. Is little red ones you must watching for. They bite. Will hurt like crikey. You want for to go swimming on other side today. No jelly fishes there. They are all go for swimmings in the bay.'

Janet laughed again, doubtfully. They had looked nasty enough, but certainly she had suffered no harm from the contact with the jellyfish.

Elena looked at her sharply. 'You getting cold,' she said. It wasn't a

70

question. 'You getting into shower. I make some hot coffee.'

Janet was not sorry to obey. After a warm shower and quick shampoo, she went to the kitchen to drink her coffee. Elena talked to her, all the time chopping up lamb and doing something with vine leaves.

Janet changed into her white dress for dinner. Her hair, freshly washed, glowed under the gentle lights. Paul, who came in late, commented, 'We'll have to buy you some more clothes.'

'Carla's sending me some money soon,' Janet said. 'I had a telephone call this morning.'

'Then we'll have a shopping spree,' Paul said. 'You'll let me help you choose them, won't you? I want to see my Janet blossom turn into the flower she was intended to be.'

'You've got much better taste than I have,' Janet said humbly.

'I'll teach you,' Paul said. 'I am an interior designer you know. It's a skill, like anything else, like typing.'

'Did you design this place?' she asked. It hadn't occurred to wonder what Paul did for a living.

'Of course.' He laughed. 'Why don't you come out and admire my patio?'

'I didn't know interior designers designed outdoor things.'

'This one does,' he said.

They sat together for a long time under the velvet sky. Later, as Janet lay in bed, luxuriating in the soft sheets and the perfume of roses, she thought how lucky she was to be here.

For a long time she lay and thought, mostly about Paul, remembering the warmth of him and the tender look in his dark eyes. She began, again, to torture herself with doubts. Why had he lied about Georgios? What was the real reason for that argument with Elena? And what about the photograph?

Her luxurious half-dream turned to troubled sleep. She tossed and turned, dozed and woke. There seemed to be a trace of light filtering through the curtains. Her hand went out to her watch, which should have been on the bedside table. She groped blindly, but couldn't locate it.

She switched on the light, but there was no watch. It wasn't on the table and she couldn't find it on the floor. Then she remembered she had taken off her watch and sun-glasses before she went for her swim, and, after the fright with the jellyfish, she had left them. They must be there now, still on the table.

She opened the shutters and peered down on to the patio below.

There was a man on the terrace. He stood, leaning against the iron railings, looking out on to the sea. He seemed, for an instant, totally relaxed and at ease, but suddenly he stiffened. For a moment he half-turned, and then, swiftly, swung back to face the sea.

'Paul?' she called softly. He did not move.

There was no possibility this time that the man was Georgios. She slipped a dressing-gown over her bare shoulders, pushed her feet into her slippers, and ran down into the dining-room. The long, french doors on to the patio were bolted, but she pulled back the bolts and opened the door.

For a moment, she stood, blinking in the moonlight. The furniture on the patio glimmered like pale ghosts in the unearthly light, and the night air was surprisingly cool after the warmth of the villa.

Janet felt cold suddenly. The figure at the railings had moved. No longer was he standing gazing tranquilly over the bay, but was in the shadows near the path. He stood absolutely motionless, his white coat a mere paleness in the shadows.

The unmistakable smell of tobacco wafted to her nostrils. That was another thing. Why hadn't she thought of it before? The man on the patio had a cigarette, and she had never seen Paul smoke.

Her heart beat faster, and beads of cold sweat began to break out on her forehead. Who was this man, lurking in the darkness? Whoever it was, he must be able to see her, framed as she was in the doorway by the light from the dining-room. She caught her breath.

The figure began to walk towards her, not quickly, but firmly. Panic-stricken, she tried to think of something heavy, a weapon. There was nothing. Then, in a flash of inspiration, her hand sought and found the switch on the door jamb, and the patio was suddenly flooded with light.

'Janet,' a voice said lightly, 'what on earth are you doing? You'll catch your death of cold.' The speaker moved forward so that his face was bathed in light.

It was Paul, an ashtray in his hand.

Torn between relief and hopelessness, Janet tumbled to the floor in a faint.

# 4

She awoke on the sofa in the front room, with Elena bending over her saying anxiously, 'Drink this, Miss Janet. You must for having somethings to drink. No, don't sit up.'

Janet sank back. Her head throbbed painfully, and when she raised her hand to her temple she discovered a huge bump, swollen and bruised.

'I think you hitted your head on somethings when you are falling,' Elena explained, pressing a cold flannel to the afflicted spot. 'You lie here, Miss Janet, and I get a rug. You sleep now, and in the morning you better. I bring you breakfast here. No workings this morning. Mr Paul, you looking after her now.'

He came to her, kneeled down, and took her hand. 'Janet,' he said, and his voice was breaking. 'Dear Janet, are you all right? Talk to me.'

Janet found her voice. 'I'm all right.'

He leaned over her, and kissed her gently, but she turned away, tears smarting behind her eyes.

'It was you,' she said, as the memories came back to her. 'The other evening. It was you. Don't try to deny it. It was.'

Paul looked at her, and his eyes were heavy with grief. He said nothing.

'Why?' she demanded, 'Why?' She half-raised her head, but the throbbing drove her back on to the pillow.

Paul stroked the small fingers. 'Oh, Janet,' he said, 'if only you knew.' He sighed. 'Perhaps — '

Elena was beside him, a rug in her arms. 'No,' she said, and there was a sharpness in her tone which made Janet look up in surprise. Elena smiled at her, reassuringly, but to Paul, she said something hastily in Greek, and there was no smile at all.

Paul sighed again, and nodded.

'You sleep now,' Elena said. 'No

more words. Your head hurt?'

'A little,' Janet said and then Elena ushered Paul away.

At the door, she turned. 'You sleep,' she said, but there was to be no sleep for Janet that night, only confused half-dreams in which Paul loved her, spurned her, and stood like a glimmering ghost in the darkness above the midnight sea.

In the morning, Paul looked tired and drawn. He drew a chair up beside the sofa. This time all Elena's protestations could not persuade him to move.

'Hello, Janet.' He looked so worn that she had not the heart to brush him aside. 'That bang on your head was very nasty. How is it now?'

'Still sore,' she said, 'but better than it was.'

Paul looked at her, and the handsome face was dark with emotion. He lifted her gently to him, and she surrendered to his arms, laying her bruised forehead against his shoulder, and weeping with great, gulping sobs.

78

'Janet, Janet,' Paul was saying. 'This should not be happening. It was not part of the plan that you should care for me, and you do, don't you?'

Janet nodded, dumbly. Paul pressed her close again. 'Janet, try to trust me. There are problems in this family — in this villa — which you couldn't begin to guess at. There are things which you can't know. Trust me, Janet. If you love me at all, trust me. At least for a little while.'

She pulled her head away and looked into his eyes. They met hers, but they were dark and troubled, and she could not read the message which was written there. 'I do trust you, Paul, I do.' There was a short pause, and then she said, fighting back the tears, 'At least, I want to.'

Paul looked earnestly into her face. 'Then, Janet, you must do as I ask you. Don't wander around the villa at night again, please.'

Her jaw dropped. This was the last thing she was expecting. 'Why?'

He shook his head. 'I can't tell you that. I wish I could, but I can't. There are too many things at stake.'

She looked at him aghast. 'It's not — anything criminal, is it, Paul?'

Paul shook his head gently. 'No,' he said, 'not criminal. Although I sometimes wonder if it is, well, quite honest.' He squeezed her hands. 'I'm sorry, Janet. I can't tell you any more.'

She looked at him with a tremulous smile. 'And it's because of this, whatever it is, that you lied to me about the other night? There was some reason why you hid in the shadows, and ran away from me?'

'My poor Janet,' Paul said. 'I know how it must have looked. But things aren't necessarily what they seem. If I appeared unkind and unfriendly, I cannot help it. Darling Janet, I wish things did not have to be this way. I wish I was free to tell you the truth, to tell you how, ever since you have been here, you have taken over my life with your sweet simplicity and your smile. I wish I was free to tell you that I love you, Janet, but I'm not, my dear. Not yet.'

He pulled her to him, and she saw Elena, over his shoulder, standing in the doorway, with a face like thunder.

★ ★ ★

Janet's enjoyment of breakfast was marred by the undercurrent of anger which she could feel between Paul and Elena.

She lay listening to their voices in the adjoining room. They were clearly arguing about something. Elena's voice rose and fell excitedly. Paul's replies were insistent and firm.

Janet sighed. Trust him, he said. It was difficult to trust anyone. The more she thought over the events of the last few days, the less she understood them. And there was always Carla.

The thought of Carla roused her into action, and she tried to rise, to get back to work, but the room swam around her and she was obliged to sink back, and was grateful to slip into sleep.

Elena woke her, coming for the tray. She smiled, but she had obviously been crying again.

'You all right, Miss Janet?' she asked. 'I think you must for staying here today. Tomorrow, workings.'

Janet was glad enough to take the advice, and for most of the morning she did nothing but doze. After lunch, for which Paul did not appear, she persuaded Elena to bring her some papers, and did a little, fitful work. Elena came in with some sewing, and for an hour or so they worked in companionable silence.

At last, Janet put aside the paragraph she was reading, and Elena looked at her and began to talk hesitantly.

'Miss Janet, is not my business what you do, but this house, that is my business.' She stopped, and the colour rushed to her cheeks. 'Is Mr Paul. Is things you do not know about Mr Paul.

I worry in my heart about these things, but last night I know I must speak with you. Miss Carla, she will be very angry if she knows.'

Janet had been afraid of that. She said nothing, and Elena went on in a rush.

'All the years, Miss Carla is careful who she send to this island. Never is pretty girl, never is for long time. But now! Oh, Miss Janet. What will Miss Carla say? This friends with Paul, it is not possible.' She looked at Janet. 'Miss Carla, she telephone this morning. She is coming soon.'

'Two weeks,' Janet said. 'A fortnight, that's what she said.'

'Miss Janet, listen to me. Wait until Miss Carla comes. See what she saying about Mr Paul. And then we see. I think if she knows, she sends you home.'

Elena folded up her sewing, and rose to her feet. 'And honest, Miss Janet, I like you. I don't want that you are sent home straight away. Mind what I say, Miss Janet. I think you must keep away from Mr Paul. I see the look on his face this morning when I come in. Is important.'

'What's important?' Paul appeared so suddenly that both women started. 'Why the glum faces? Elena, what have you been saying to our invalid?'

With an effort Janet found her voice. 'Elena was just telling me that it was important for me to rest,' she said, a little unsteadily.

Elena looked at her sharply, but said nothing.

'She's quite right. This bump on my head is very painful. I think I'll take life quietly for a day or two. I'll have my dinner in here, Elena, and go to bed early.'

Paul looked disappointed. 'Oh, Janet, I was looking forward to your company. And I wanted to take you shopping tomorrow. I've got to go to Spetse town all day. Won't you come?'

Janet shook her head, trying not to let the misery show on her face. 'No,' she said. 'This head is worse than I thought. And, since I haven't done much today, if I'm feeling better, I'd really better catch up.'

Paul smiled and came over, dropping a kiss on her hair. He stood by the sofa, looking down at her. Janet found it hard to imagine anything sinister in the beautiful, dark eyes, but she remembered Elena's words.

'Paul,' she whispered, 'I'd love to come to Spetse town with you, but I've got to do what Carla wants done.'

Paul bowed his head, and sighed, but when he raised his eyes again there was a bitterness in them which Janet had never seen before.

'What Carla wants. Yes, naturally.' He gave a short laugh. 'What Carla wants comes first. It always does. It always did.' He left the room, slamming the door behind him. He didn't come in for dinner.

★ ★ ★

For the next few days, Janet avoided Paul. She took her meals in the study, and Paul did not come to trouble her. She saw him, fleetingly, through the windows, standing at the wheel of the yacht, but the great boat never budged from its moorings and when she looked again, Paul had gone.

Elena came and went, quietly carrying meals. Once or twice she hovered, as if she would be happy to talk, but Janet only smiled and said, 'That'll be all. Thank you, Elena,' and the girl went back to the kitchen looking unhappy. Janet did not feel forgiving. If she could not talk to Paul, she would talk to nobody. She buried herself in her work. The book would be ready for Carla's arrival.

Only in the afternoons did Janet permit herself the luxury of a long, cool swim. She could lie back in the luxurious, cool depths, and forget — or almost forget. Her daily swim did wonders for her spirits.

There were other effects from her

swim, too. Her shoulders were touched with honey. Her skin darkened into a warm, glowing tan, and the daily exercise gave her grace and shapeliness. Unknown to herself, Janet grew more beautiful daily.

One afternoon Elena came to the study. Janet was sorting the manuscript, which was spread out on the floor around her. Elena came in cautiously, picking her way among the papers.

'I sorry to disturb, Miss Janet, but I must to know what things you are wanting for dinner tomorrow and next day.'

Janet frowned. Usually Elena simply prepared the meals and served them. If she discussed them with anyone it was presumably Paul. 'I don't know, Elena,' she said. 'Whatever you think.'

'But Miss Janet,' Elena persisted, 'is Friday.'

Janet stared at her for a moment in bewilderment. Then realisation dawned. Friday. Elena would be going home for the weekend. She would be alone in the villa. Alone with Paul. Her mind whirled with delight and dismay.

'Can have chickens,' Elena went on, 'or lamb. What you like. Or I see what best things in market. Georgios is taking me now to town.'

'Do that, Elena,' Janet said. 'Only no octopus.'

Elena smiled. 'All right. I go.' But she didn't go. Instead, she stood awkwardly, shifting her weight from one foot to the other. 'Miss Janet,' she burst out. 'I sorry if I upset you. Only I think that when Miss Carla come, she will send you away, and there will be much sadness. I not want you to be hurted in your heart.' She stopped, uncomfortably, and then said, 'I didn't want for you to sit in here all days.'

The apology was so freely given that Janet could not resist it.

'It's all right, Elena,' she said. 'Don't worry about it. I'm all right. I'm going to go and have a swim, right now.'

Elena smiled gratefully. 'I glad, Miss Janet. You enjoy your swimmings.'

'I ought to go to Spetse town with you,' Janet said, 'and buy myself a new swimming costume. Mine's an old one, and it's beginning to fall apart. Look!' She picked up the costume from the chair where it lay waiting for her afternoon swim, and stretched the strap as she spoke. As she did so, the material parted and the strap tore in two.

Elena looked at her for a moment, and then said eagerly, 'I knowing what, Miss Janet. I got a swimming costume in my room, you borrow him.'

Janet began to protest, but Elena went on, 'No, no, is good for you — your colour. Miss Carla give me, but not good fits. I think it fit you good.'

Elena was right — the costume fitted perfectly, and Janet had to admit that the shocking, sapphire-blue suited her wonderfully.

'Is this, too,' Elena said, producing a blue swimming cap. 'You putting that on, too. Keeping your hair dry.'

Janet, reluctantly, allowed herself to be persuaded and headed for the sea.

She dived expertly off the jetty and then rounded the headland with a few swift strokes into the sheltered waters of what she had christened Jellyfish Bay. The tranquil seclusion of the spot attracted her, and, around the corner, out of sight of the villa, she could rid herself of that ridiculous cap.

The tide was in and she hauled herself up on to the welcoming, warm surface of one of the flat rocks, and sat for a moment revelling in the sunshine, the scenery and the sea.

Suddenly, she felt a movement behind her, and a pair of strong arms encircled her. Warm lips were kissing her shoulder, and a voice said, 'Did you think you could avoid me so easily?'

Janet spun round, to find herself in the arms of a total stranger.

There was a long, awkward silence, during which neither of them moved. He was young, tall, muscular and bronzed, with a fringe of fair hair which tumbled over a boyish face. Janet looked at him in wonder. Three weeks ago, if fate had placed her in the arms of such a man, she would have blessed her destiny.

Her face was a portrait of amazement, and Janet realised that her jaw had dropped. She shut her mouth firmly, and said, ridiculously, 'I'm sorry.'

'No. I'm sorry,' the young man said, releasing her.

'American?' Janet asked in amazement.

'Well, sort of. I haven't been in the States for three or four years now. I found this little island and fell in love with it. I've kinda settled here.'

'Doing what?' The conversation seemed natural, as though they'd known each other for years.

'Oh, lotus-eating, I guess. It's a good life if you don't weaken.' He stretched out beside her on the rock, young muscles gleaming with sunshine and sea water. 'What about you? We don't have too many new faces around here.'

'I'm working here,' Janet said primly. 'As a secretary.'

'Really?' He sounded interested. 'Been here long?'

'No, not really,' she replied.

'No wonder I haven't seen you before. I've been off the island for a fortnight. English, are you?'

Janet nodded.

'Here, I'm sorry if I scared you back there a minute ago. I thought — ' He groaned. 'I really am sorry.'

'You thought I was someone else,' Janet supplied. To her relief a broad grin spread over his face.

'As a matter of fact, I did. I saw you from out back, and you look mighty like the lady. Same clothes I've seen her wear. And I thought — well, it's kinda hard to explain. You wouldn't understand.'

'Try me,' Janet said, taking off the ridiculous blue cap. In her heart she was secretly amused. Another of Carla's muscular, young men. It was funny really, mistaking her for Carla.

'Go on then, tell me. I think you owe me an explanation at least.'

He laughed, blushing a little. 'Sure, maybe you're right. Seems a little impolite to say to a lady that you kissed her because you thought you were kissing somebody else. But, well it's like this. I used to come here with, well, with this friend of mine, and I thought she was getting kind of fond of me. I told her how I felt about her, and she just up and left me. Never saw her again. I came here most days, but she never showed up. Then I saw you, and I thought, well, I guess, you know what I thought.'

'You thought she'd come back,' Janet finished for him.

'Yes, ma'am, I sure did. I thought she'd come back,' the man repeated, staring out to sea, with a hurt, puzzled face.

Poor boy, Janet thought. How like Carla, teasing, flattering, leading him on, trifling with his affections. Her heart went out to the young man with the broken dreams. 'Well, she hasn't,' she said, and was aware that it sounded unkind. 'I'm sorry I wasn't your young lady — er, I don't know your name.'

'I'm Joe,' he said. 'My full name is Joseph Seymore Winterbourne, Junior.'

'Winterbourne?' The name rang bells in Janet's mind, bells that spoke of a fortune in computers.

'Winterbourne,' he repeated, in a voice which did not invite further enquiry. 'Round here they call me Joe.'

'And I'm Janet Lister,' Janet told him.

'Well, hi, Janet,' Joe said. Janet began to laugh. 'What's up?' he asked, half-laughing himself.

'I was just thinking,' Janet said. 'Usually a man introduces himself, tells you his life story and then he kisses you. Not the other way round.'

'It isn't often that you kiss the wrong girl by mistake.' Joe smiled ruefully. 'But that swimsuit is awful like the one she used to wear.'

Janet smiled. 'I think I'd better tell

you, Joe. I think it probably is the one she used to wear. I work up at the villa. This was Carla's bathing costume. She gave it to someone who lent it to me. No wonder you were confused.'

'No,' Joe was saying stupidly. 'No, it was silly. You're taller and fairer and slimmer than — '

'Joe,' she interrupted, 'Oh, Joe. You thought I was Elena!'

He nodded. 'I know,' he said. 'She's only up there working, but who the heck cares about that? I don't. I know I'm a Winterbourne and all that, but if I love her, what's the difference? If she doesn't like the business, I could stay here, buy a few apartments, let them to tourists. Lots of Greek men here have English wives. Why not the other way round?'

'And she won't marry you because of your family?' Janet asked. This was a new view of Elena.

'Darned if I know.' Joe ran a huge hand through the ragged, blonde fringe. 'It seemed more like she was frightened of something. I thought maybe her family didn't like to think of their girl getting mixed up with a foreigner. I went to see her father, hoping I could talk him round, make him see things my way — '

'And you couldn't?' Janet supplied.

'He warned me off,' Joe's voice was full of mystification. 'That's just about the way of it. He was polite enough, but the message was clear.' He turned to Janet, a worried look in his eyes. 'Janet, I'll level with you. You work up at that villa. You know the set-up. You tell me. Do you think she's mixed up in something up there? Seems to me, everyone is mightily anxious to keep me away from her all of a sudden.'

'And you haven't seen her since?' Janet queried.

'I've seen her a couple of times. I used to bring my boat here. She slipped out and swam round to meet me. She wore that swimsuit. Then, one day, she told me she couldn't meet me anymore.' He turned to Janet, his eyes full of pain. 'Something about the family. She said she couldn't tell me any more. She told me to go back to America and find some nice girl to marry.'

'How long ago was that?' Janet asked.

'Six, seven months now, near enough,' Joe said.

'And you kept coming?'

'Most days. Though, like I said, I get away off the island for a week or two now and then.'

'But what about Elena? She goes home Fridays. Can't you see her then?'

'I've tried, but on the weekend her family are all around her. Never met people so wrapped up in families. Just around the time she came to work here someone died. Her sister I think. Maybe that's got something to do with it. I figured she was keeping away because she — well, out of respect to her sister, but I don't know. Nobody will tell me anything. Perhaps it's just my family, like she said. Maybe it's her family. But I think it's something up there in that villa. What gives, up there, Janet? What's the secret?'

Janet sat for a moment in silence. Should she talk to this unknown young man with the fresh face and the troubled eyes? Somehow, she trusted him. He, too, loved someone who was cut off from him by the mysterious secret which surrounded the villa. She took a deep breath and began to tell him the story.

When she had finished, he looked at her glumly.

'Seems to me it's the same story again. You think something's not right, I think something's not right.' He stretched out a strong right arm and dabbled it in the water. 'I'm half afraid, to tell you the truth, Janet. Is there somebody else? Is there a man she sees up at the villa?'

'Oh, no,' Janet said lightly. 'Nobody at all. There's only me and Paul — ' Even as she said the words, she realised the possibility behind them. Elena and Paul? Surely not. What man could sit under the stars with one girl, while another girlfriend washed the dishes not fifty yards away?

'Paul? That's Paul Stavropolous, isn't it?' Joe asked.

Janet nodded.

'Huh,' he said, shortly, 'I suppose it's possible. Though it can't be for his money. Stavropolous may be a millionaire, but the Winterbournes could probably buy him out two or three times over. Why, I remember — '

'Stavropolous a millionaire?' Janet couldn't believe her ears.

'Didn't you know?' Joe's voice was incredulous. 'How do you think he could afford a villa like that one, a motor-boat, a yacht. And there's an apartment in Rome, too, I understand.'

'I thought it was Carla's house.'

'Carla's? No, no. The Stavropolous family have lived on Spetse for hundreds of years. This house is new, of course. Designed it himself, folks say.'

Oh, yes, Janet knew about that. 'He told me he was an interior designer,' she said in a small voice.

'That so? That what he does now?' Joe's voice was totally uninterested. 'I knew he'd retired from the movies. Stavropolous was one of the all-time greats in the Greek movies business. A marvellous actor, so they say. Then he suddenly jacked it all in, and went into retirement.'

'I thought you said no-one told you anything,' Janet said.

'I didn't have to ask anyone about that. I knew already. Time was, they used to point out the Stavropolous house from the tourist ferries. Mind you,' he went on, suddenly serious, 'they don't do that any more, either. He hasn't had his picture in the Greek papers for years.' Joe paused. 'Not since that big wedding. When's she coming home, anyway?'

'Who?' Janet said blankly. The world seemed to be spinning around her.

'Why, your boss. The redheaded lady, the writer. Carla whatever she called herself. His wife, Mrs Stavropolous . . . '

# 5

There was, it seemed, no doubt about it. The wedding had been in all the papers. The beautiful, wealthy English writer and the matinée idol. That must have been when Janet saw them on television. Joe was quite certain. Elena had shown him the photographs, when they first met. 'There was some family connection, she said.' Joe's face cleared. 'I'd totally forgotten that about family connections. I knew the family would be behind this. It isn't like Elena. She loves me, I know she does, and no family is going to come between us.'

Janet heard his words as if they came from outer space. Mrs Stavropolous. Carla was Mrs Stavropolous. No wonder there was a connecting door into her bedroom from Paul's apartments.

'She calls herself Mrs Ryder,' she said to Joe, in a voice which had become thin and faraway. 'Not Stavropolous.'

'Perhaps it's her pen name,' Joe said. His mind was on other things.

Janet shivered, and at once Joe was on his feet, all concern.

'You're cold. Come on, I'll row you round to the jetty.'

She declined his offer and slipped back into the friendly water where the salt water from her tears could mingle unnoticed with the sea.

When she got back to the villa, the motor-boat had gone. Elena had left for town. Janet would have liked to talk to her, to tell her about Joe. Much more than that, she wanted to ask about Carla and Paul, but the villa was empty.

Janet tried to go back to work, but it was impossible.

She wandered around the villa, gazing from every window hoping to glimpse the returning motor-boat but the shadows lengthened, and the afternoon limped slowly by without a sign of it. At last, Janet abandoned herself to her unhappiness, and flung herself face downward on the sofa, weeping.

A soft touch on her arm roused her. She swung round. Paul was standing over her. He stooped, letting an armful of parcels and boxes tumble to the floor as he gathered her to him and covered her tear-stained face with burning kisses.

'Janet,' he murmured thickly. 'Janet, my love. What is it?'

At the words, her tears began again, and he held her unresisting until the fit of weeping passed.

'Now,' he said, seizing both her hands, as if she were a small child. 'Tell me all about it.'

The words were chocked with tears, but she managed to stammer out, 'I heard — I found out — I didn't know about your wife.'

'Oh, Janet.' He tipped her face backward and looked deep into her eyes. 'Elena has been talking to you?'

'Yes,' she admitted, 'and I met

someone. A man down on the beach — '

'A man? What man? What did he look like?' Paul demanded.

'Young, blonde. He had a little boat. He came from the town.' She didn't betray Joe's confidences about Elena.

'Oh, I thought perhaps you had run into someone here, on the property. I thought — I don't know. There are some funny people around.' His arms went around her again, and his lips nestled against her ear. 'Poor, little Janet. Does it upset you so?'

She blinked at him, astonished. 'But Paul, I couldn't have — I wouldn't have fallen in love with you if I'd known about your wife.'

Paul looked at her with eyes that spoke volumes of tenderness. 'But, darling, darling Janet. Don't you understand? That's over, it's past. We had our happiness, yes, but that time has gone. It's time to start again. You cannot live your whole life carrying a dead love next to your heart.'

'Over?' Janet breathed. 'Really over. You mean that?'

Paul took her to him, and his lips sought her trembling ones. 'That is exactly what I mean,' he murmured.

'But Elena says — '

'I know what Elena says,' Paul interrupted, and there was a slight edge to his voice. 'She's said it to me, too. You must have heard us arguing. I know she wanted you to keep away from me. It's the Greek way. She thinks marriages are for ever, but some, some were not meant to be that way. And the only thing to do, my Janet, is to pick up the pieces and to start again. I am a lucky man, because you were there to love me — no, don't argue, you told me so yourself, a moment ago — to love me, and for me to love.' His swift arms enfolded her again, and his urgent kisses raised her own passion. They kissed as if time were precious, and they had a lifetime of separation to make up for.

At last he let her go. 'And I do love

you, Janet,' Paul said.

Paul had plans for that evening. He was taking her to a barbecue at a beach taverna on the other side of town. 'Elena wasn't very pleased,' Paul said teasingly, 'until I reminded her that Georgios would be there, too. Then it was suddenly all right.'

'I must get changed,' Janet said, surveying her dress in dismay. She had slipped the white dress over her swimming costume and it was crumpled and damp. 'Or I could rinse it through.' There was almost enough time for it to dry in the evening breeze.

'Nonsense,' Paul said firmly. 'You wouldn't go to Spetse town with me, so I had to bring your dresses to you.' He stooped to pick up some of the larger boxes at his feet. 'Go on,' he urged, as her hand hovered over the string. 'Open it. And no grumbles,' he added. 'I can afford it.'

The dresses were beautiful. There were four of them, each simply cut, and the colours were cool and pure, far from the insipid designs she had always chosen. She loved them on sight.

There were sandals, too, and a bracelet, understated but beautiful. Janet guessed it was real silver. She hesitated, but Paul, sensitive as ever to her moods, said, 'Part of the design. Go on then, model them for me.'

She did so with delight. Paul adjusted a collar here, a waist band there, and finally, he took her hair and wound it in a thick rope over one shoulder. 'The loveliest girl in Greece,' he murmured. He tipped her head back gently, and his eyes burned with longing. 'Janet, I must go and change. Georgios will be waiting for us, and I cannot bear to be so close and so alone, and not to touch you. Wait here for me, I shan't be long.'

She stood on the patio after he had gone, watching the lights from the boathouse reflecting back from the violet sea. A touch of make-up was the only change she made to herself.

'Miss Lister.' Georgios clambered up

the track, his swarthy, handsome face wreathed in smiles 'Boat is ready. You coming now?' He stopped, gazing at her. 'Is a beautiful dress, Miss Lister.'

Janet smiled nervously. She heard a step on the path, and there was the handsome, white-coated figure of Paul, crossing the patio.

'Isn't she lovely, Georgios? And she's with me. Come on then, let's go. The night is young.'

The night was very old before they returned to the villa, a night of laughter, of Greek wine, of strangely haunting music; a great ram roasted over an open fire, which melted in delicious tenderness in the mouth; a night of dancing and wine.

Afterwards, the world seemed very joyous, and a little unsteady, and she was glad of Paul's arm around her waist, and his shoulder seemed very comfortable. She was still smiling when Paul laid her gently on her bed, and tiptoed from the room, leaving her to sleep.

She deserved a headache, but next day, Paul produced a remedy which must have been excellent, because by lunchtime she was ready for the delicious salad which Elena had left prepared, and the afternoon was devoted to a cruise around the island in Paul's yacht.

Janet had never been in a sailing boat before, not even a dinghy, and the mass of ropes and pulleys alarmed her. She realised, too, that the day was somehow a turning point for Paul. And when, a little way from the jetty, Paul stopped the engine, and the great, white mainsail fluttered up and took the breeze, she was in an enchantment of fear and delight. The boat leaned slightly into the wind, and the proud bow rose and fell, screaming across the emerald water, while Janet sat, hunched with excitement, watching the water, the island and her love.

They sailed right around the island, anchored off a small bay, and swam lazily side by side in the deep, limpid waters. They drifted past the harbour and glimpsed the bustle that was Spetse town, and saw the hydrofoil, raised up on its hind legs like some speeding insect, hunting across the open water.

'Two hours to Athens,' Paul said. 'But who'd want to be in Athens?' His arm tightened around her and her world was complete.

That night, with Paul's kisses still burning on her lips, Janet could not sleep for several hours, for excitement and happiness. It had been so wonderful. Almost too good to be true, she thought dreamily, and slipped finally into sleep.

Outside on the patio, a solitary figure stood, smoking a cigarette and staring thoughtfully and sadly out across the starlit sea . . .

* * *

At breakfast, Janet's thoughts were as sunny as the morning. She sat with Paul on the patio, until the telephone

110

interrupted their lazy breakfast.

'I'll get it,' Janet said.

Paul stood up and looked down at her with the dark eyes she had learned to love. 'No,' he said lightly. 'I'll go. It might be business. Don't move. You look so lovely with the sunshine in your hair. I won't be long.'

Janet waited. Five minutes became ten. Quarter of an hour lengthened into half an hour. Janet stirred restlessly. Surely he couldn't still be on the telephone?

She began to collect the breakfast dishes, and took them back to the kitchen. Still Paul did not appear. A little hurt, she made her way to the study. Paul's voice, friendly and laughing came to her, still on the telephone. Reassured, she turned to tiptoe back to the patio, but Paul's next sentence stopped her. It was her own name.

'Yes,' Paul was saying, 'Janet's here. She's having breakfast at the moment.' There was a pause, then Paul laughed, rather nastily, and said, 'Yes, she's worked hard, I'll grant you that, but in my life she's nothing but a nuisance.'

Janet stood transfixed, unable to believe her own ears.

'I don't know what's in her head,' Paul went on, and there was real irritation in his voice. 'I get the impression she sees herself settling down here and becoming Mrs Stavropolous. Almost wish she would. It would be very convenient from my point of view. At least my position would be clearer, and I could start living again. What's that? I couldn't bear to share the villa with her permanently?' He sighed. 'I don't know. I've been thinking about that, but on the whole I think it's a small price to pay. She's entertaining in her own way. And after all, if she was settled here, I wouldn't have to stay here myself all the time, would I?'

There was a long pause. Janet held her breath, unable to move. Paul said something which she did not catch, and then laughed again, a knowing, conspiratorial laugh.

'Naturally,' he said to the unknown voice on the telephone. 'We'll have to humour her. I've already done everything in my power to please, but I can't keep it up for ever. Sooner or later it'll have to stop. I can't keep on pretending.'

In the corridor, Janet continued to listen, in a kind of daze. There was more, about the island, about Georgios, about Elena, and then Paul said, 'It's not very easy for me either. How do you think I feel when I read the newspaper reports, 'Carla Ryder dines with millionaire playboy.' How am I supposed to feel? I know the truth, of course, but it's very upsetting for all that.' He laughed uneasily. 'There's something I wanted to ask you. It's about Janet.'

Janet could feel her heart pounding against her ribs. All shame forgotten, she listened, straining to catch every word.

But Paul merely said, more gently,

'Yes, all right. I won't do anything until you come. When exactly were you expecting to arrive? As soon as that? No! No! No problem. The sooner we can get this over with, the better. Yes, of course I can come to the airport and get you, nothing I'd like more. We can talk then about how to handle things as far as Janet is concerned. Don't take too long about it, though. My patience isn't unlimited. And now I must get back to Janet. She's waiting on the patio.'

Janet had just time to pull herself together, and retreat slightly, before Paul opened the door of the study, and came towards her, his arms outstretched.

'Oh, Janet,' he said. Did she imagine it, or was the tenderness in the voice forced? 'Did I keep you waiting, Janet? I'm sorry, my love, but something has happened.'

'Happened? What?' Janet scarcely knew what she was saying.

'It's Carla,' Paul was saying lightly.

'She's coming tomorrow. She and Steve.'

Tears sprang to Janet's eyes, and Paul smiled at her gently. 'Not jealous, Janet?' he said teasingly. 'Surely you can bear to share me with Carla.'

She had no answer, but shook her head tearfully and escaped into the study. Paul followed her.

'Oh, come on, Janet,' he coaxed. 'This is our last day alone before they come — let's enjoy it. A picnic? A swim? What do you fancy?'

Janet found her voice and pleaded that, if Carla was returning, she must devote the day to work. 'I'll eat in here,' she blurted. 'That way I won't be distracted.'

'You know best,' Paul said in a hurt, puzzled voice. 'If you change your mind, I'll be on the boat.'

But she didn't change her mind. She stayed in the study, making the file of manuscripts a kind of defence behind which she could hide from Paul. Yet she could not hide from her thoughts, nor from the recollection of that telephone call. What did it mean, she wondered, and found herself no answer.

Her heart was still set pounding by the memory of his kisses, but then she would remember his words, 'I can't keep it up much longer.' Was it all a pretence, part of some deep scheme which she didn't understand. Was that why, on the patio, he had been so evasive?

It was just as well she had done her work on the manuscript earlier. Today she could do no more than turn the pages.

She ate no lunch. Paul came in at dinner time and tried to tempt her to eat, but she took only some fresh fruit and cheese, and went to bed early.

She drifted at last into an uneasy rest, then sat up suddenly, startled into wakefulness. There it was again. Paul's voice raised in anger or emotion. 'I'm sorry, but I can't go on like this. I've had enough!'

Had she dreamt it? The words seemed to ring in the air, but there was no sound now, nothing but a fierce rattle of the shutters, and the hammering of rain.

'I'm imagining things,' Janet said aloud, but she could not convince herself.

'Trust me,' Paul had said, but it was time, Janet decided, that he told her the truth. She had overheard the telephone conversation almost without meaning to. Very well, she would tell him so. Tomorrow, first thing, she would confront him, tell him about her fears. Perhaps there was some rational explanation. The last time, when she had distrusted him, she had only to ask him and he'd explained about his marriage. She would ask him, first thing in the morning. And, soothing her restless mind with that thought, she slept, while the storm whistled on . . .

Her first thought on waking was that the usual morning sunlight was not filtering through the shutters. Surprised, she opened them and gazed out on the now beloved and familiar island. Grey drizzle dripped from a grey sky, and a fitful wind shivered the olive trees and stripped the tattered petals from the blossoms. Beyond the empty jetty, the sea disappeared in a grey mist.

The empty jetty. It was a moment before the realisation sank in. The yacht, she knew, was in the boathouse, but the motor-boat? It had been there last night. She had seen it from the window, as she struggled with misery and jealousy amongst Carla's manuscripts.

She seized a wrap and pulled it on, then raced out through the house, and down the winding path to the sea. It was hard to know what she expected to find.

She walked out on to the jetty, taking great care, because the surface was slippery with green and brown fronds. Something cold and soft moved beneath her heel. Jellyfish! The red jellyfish which Elena had warned her 'hurt like crikey.' It seemed the last straw, and she picked her way forlornly back to the villa.

When she pushed back the french doors and slipped into the dining-room, her mood lifted. The table was laid for breakfast, a scent of hot coffee and new bread was in the air, and from the kitchen came a cheerful whistle.

'Paul.' Janet's cry was joyful. Heedless now of her dripping clothes she burst into the kitchen, a cry of welcome on her lips, and new hope in her heart. She would ask him, he would explain. The whole, grey morning seemed suddenly brighter.

'Good-morning, Miss Janet. Every-things are nearly ready for your breakfast. Is my brother in the kitchen? I sorry for the noise.' Elena stood in the doorway, a pot of steaming coffee in her hands. 'Mr Paul, he was went already for the airport. He telling me to be letting you sleep, and here you are already being an early worm this morning.' She smiled happily.

'Everythings is OK with you?'

Janet nodded dumbly, but her tears were close to falling.

The coffee was excellent, and the rolls and coffee melted in the mouth, but Janet ate them mechanically, as though she was swallowing dry bread and water. Her stomach still lurched treacherously at the memory of yesterday morning and that phone call.

'Anythings the matter?' Elena asked anxiously.

'No, no,' Janet lied. 'It's lovely.' And she took another roll, and broke it into tiny pieces on her plate.

Elena was not so easily convinced. She disappeared into the kitchen and returned with a glass of orange juice for Janet.

'Miss Janet,' she said firmly, 'somethings is wrong. All in a sudden you don't eating, you don't talking, you don't working. Last week I told to you some things, and I think you are cross to me. The same things I tell to Mr Paul, and he is cross to me. I don't want for making you unhappy, Miss Janet. I think perhaps I should to shut my mouth and to say nothing. I am very sorry, Miss Janet.'

Janet saw that there was genuine distress in Elena's voice, and she wanted very much to comfort the girl. She tried to speak calmly. 'It's all right, Elena. It's something else, something I heard yesterday.'

Elena said nothing, but she nodded sympathetically. She still held the glass of orange juice. Janet looked at the girl's kind, open face, and suddenly made a decision. She would confide in Elena. On this strange island she felt so confused and alone.

'I don't know what to do, Elena,' she said all in a rush. 'I came here to work, and, well, to forget someone. That can be hard to do sometimes.' Amazingly she realised she had succeeded. She had not thought of David for days.

'I know,' Elena said in a small, sad voice. 'But then, you have met Mr Paul, and is easy to forget, I think?'

'I'm afraid so.'

Elena smiled. 'Is all right, Miss Janet. Is natural. Mr Paul is very nice, very rich man. Very handsome. Is only, I think he also forgetting very quickly.'

Janet nodded. 'I know. Only you see, when I came here to work for Carla, I didn't know about — I didn't realise.' She was going to say that Carla was married to Paul but the words hurt too much and she stuttered, 'I didn't know that Carla was married. At least, I thought she was Mrs Ryder. I didn't know that she was Mrs Stavropolous. I didn't know about that.'

'You find out?' Elena seemed very agitated. 'I didn't talk to you about it.'

'No, of course you didn't,' Janet said. 'I saw a photograph once in England, but I didn't know he was her husband.'

Elena sank down in the deep chair, and began to drink the orange juice. It occurred to Janet much later that that simple act was an indication of how upset Elena was.

'No, Miss Carla, she keep it a big secret since — since — what happen.'

'What did happen, exactly?' Janet said gently. Why should anybody want to keep their marriage such a secret, she wondered.

'Nobodies told to you what happen? Then I not tell to you. Is Miss Carla's husband, you must ask Miss Carla. I promise to her that I never telling anyone about it. She want to protect him from all newspapers coming here, take photographs, ask questions. Always she smile, dress nice, go in public, and work. You, Miss Janet, you know how hard she work, but in her head is always one thing. Always her husband. I think she love him very much, in spite of everythings.'

It was what Janet had feared most to hear.

'Does she?'

'Oh, yes, Miss Janet. She love him like crikey. He want her to leave him, is always saying is not a fair thing, this marriage. He must to stay here, he cannot go around the world like once. He want her to go away and leave him, but she don't want. She say no, keep it big secret, one day perhaps, all things be fixed again. Then can be happy. I don't know. I don't think is possible. Is too difficult.'

Janet's voice was a whisper. 'And what does Paul think about it?'

'I don't know Miss Janet. I think he think sometimes yes, sometimes no. He stay here for pleasing Miss Carla, try to help for fixing things, but I think he not stay much longer. He was unhappy, Miss Janet, until you have came. When he marry, he young, he laughs, he all time smiling, and then after what happen — Crikeys, Miss Janet, perhaps Elena should to shut mouth and say nothings to you. I don't know.' She drained the orange juice unhappily.

'I see,' Janet said quietly.

'I talking too much,' Elena said, getting to her feet. 'Is things to do. Miss Carla come home today, and she like to eat special Greek chicken, and I must for go Spetse town and buy. Mr Steve like especially this.'

'And Steve knows all about Carla's marriage?' Janet said half to herself. Of course he must know. Steve, who obviously worshipped Carla, yet always knowing that here, on Spetse, her husband waited, his photograph in the desk as a constant reminder.

'Oh, yes, Mr Steve knows. He have come to the wedding. He was went to school with Mr Paul. Is a long time he has been friend to the family, but is not many people knows this story. Is surprise for me that Mr Paul has told you.'

'Paul didn't tell me,' Janet said. 'I found out.'

Elena stared at her in amazement.

'I was told by a young man I met swimming,' Janet went on. 'A young man called Joe Winterbourne.'

It was just as well Elena had drunk the fruit juice. The glass fell from her hand and shattered on the tiled floor.

# 6

'You seen Joe?' Elena asked, her eyes sparkling with sudden light. 'Where was he?'

'He was in the cove,' Janet said. 'He thought I was you. He recognised the bathing costume.'

'Oh.' There was a long silence. 'What did he say?'

'He told me he went to the cove nearly every day, looking for you. He thinks you are avoiding him. Are you?'

Elena didn't answer. Then she said, 'He has came to the cove to find me? You are sure, Miss Janet?'

'Quite sure. He's been coming a long time, looking for you.'

'Is a long time,' Elena agreed. 'What he said when he think he talking to me?' she added shyly.

'He kissed you,' Janet said gravely. 'He came up behind you and asked if you really thought you could get away.'

'My father wrong,' Elena said. 'He say Joe is very rich American, and he not interested in Greek girl from Spetse. But more than six months, and Joe is still come to the cove for finding me. I think, perhaps, is serious, isn't it?'

'I think so,' Janet said softly, 'but he is very hurt, Elena. One day you seemed to love him, the next day you left him alone, without any explanation. He thinks it's something to do with the villa.'

'Is true, a little. Everythings happening then. Miss Carla have this big problem. My sister is die, and this make me very sad. I must to stay here and look after Mr Paul. He very sad, too. He don't eat, don't sleep. My father is saying, this Joe, he is millionaire like Stavropolous. See how unlucky all this money makes. He's saying I cannot to be friendly with Joe when my sister is just die. So I saying no, I not meeting

Joe any more, and I coming to live here and looking after all this family, and especially keeping very secret for Miss Carla.'

'It was good of you to be so loyal to Carla.'

'Miss Carla, she very kind to me when my sister is die,' Elena said, her eyes shining. 'And Mr Stavropolous, he try so hard to help her — and — '

Tears began to tumble down Elena's cheeks. Janet felt embarrassed and oddly humble. It was hard to think that anyone in the world would have cared so much if anything had happened to Janet. 'It's all right,' she managed awkwardly, although it clearly wasn't.

'I sorry, Miss Janet,' Elena said resolutely. 'I must not to cry. But is sure I must help Miss Carla and her husband, any way that I can. And Mr Paul always was so good and loving to my sister.' She sniffed back the tears. 'There, now I am better. And I am glad in my heart that Joe is coming still.'

'He wants to see you,' Janet said.

'I think I must speak to my father about this.' Elena bent down abruptly and began to collect the pieces of glass. Then she said suddenly, 'What you think of Joe, Miss Janet?'

'I thought he was lovely,' Janet said warmly.

'Yes, is what I think.' Elena rose to her feet, her cheeks pink with pleasure. 'I think I speak to my father today. I must for go to Spetse town and buying chickens for Miss Carla.'

The day dragged unendurably once Elena had left, clinging to the back of her brother as they braved the slopes on his motor-bike. Janet spent an hour or more rearranging and checking the already immaculate filmscript. She toyed with a little cheese and salad for lunch. Elena returned, in a cloud of oil and smoke, and instantly disappeared into the kitchen.

The afternoon was worse. Janet swam, despite the rain, conscious only of the thousand, unanswered questions which hammered in her brain.

Carla was coming. Carla who still loved her husband. And Paul was returning. Paul who swore his marriage was dead, who had said, only yesterday, that he loved her. What was the truth?

\* \* \*

Carla's presence filled the villa from the first moment.

As soon as the boat touched the jetty, Carla leaped ashore, elegant in cream and gold, and swung up the path to the villa with Steve. Paul struggled behind with the suitcases. Carla came straight inside and stretched out on the couch calling for coffee, gin, hot water, a bath and clean clothes.

Elena bobbed about with a joy which was obviously genuine, and somehow managed to provide all these conflicting wants at once.

Carla blew her a kiss. 'Darling Elena, you're an angel,' she cooed and disappeared into her room amid clouds of sweet-scented steam.

'Dinner in half an hour, Miss Carla,' Elena beamed.

Janet, who had said very little, and who had been greeted only by a cool, 'Good-evening, Janet,' went to her own room. Stretched out on the bed, she heard the unmistakable click of a door shutting, and the dark, pleased laugh of a man. Only then did she remember the door from Paul's apartments and realise that Paul and the suitcases had not come up to the house.

She leaped up from the bed in agitation. Anything was better than sitting alone while Carla and Paul — what? She did not dare to think. Her eyes were reddened, and she washed them with cool water before she went down to the dining-room. Steve was there, a gin and tonic in his hand.

'I must say the island seems to agree with you,' he said, and then, smiling shyly, continued, 'You've positively blossomed.'

'Yes, hasn't she?' Paul was at the french windows. It was only moments since she had heard the voices in Carla's room. Perhaps after all he had only gone there with the suitcases. It was much quicker than climbing the whole way up to the patio doors. What could be more natural? Hoping against hope, she smiled at him. He looked at her with such tenderness and pride that her knees melted, and even Steve seemed aware of it.

'All your doing, Paul, I've no doubt.' He grinned. 'Well, good luck to you. I was just about to offer the lady a drink. Want one?'

They were all sipping their drinks when Carla arrived, radiant and relaxed. Elena came in at almost the same time to announce dinner.

Elena's cooking was always excellent. Tonight it was superb. Paul said little, but ate with obvious enjoyment. Steve lost himself in the succulent feast. Janet, ill at ease, said nothing. It was left to Carla to carry the conversation.

She was entertaining, enthusiastic, but as the meal progressed Janet became aware of a certain tension. Something in the way she looked at Paul, and from Paul to Janet, showed that her mind was not wholly on the flow of stories, and as the dessert was served, and then the cheese, her animation seemed to ebb, and she spoke less and less. By the time coffee was on the table an uncomfortable silence had settled.

Carla turned to Janet. 'Well, Miss Lister, I can see that you have been doing more than typewriting. Has Paul been keeping you amused? I'm sure he's been delighted to do it.'

'Carla!' Paul's voice was sharp.

Carla smiled, but it was not a pleasant smile. 'There seems to me to have been quite a transformation. Our ugly duckling has blossomed into a swan.'

'I'm glad you approve.' Paul's voice was even.

'It's pity I wasn't here to witness the butterfly spreading its wings,' Carla went on in a brittle voice. 'I think I

should have found it very interesting.'
She looked at Paul with eyes which
were hard with anger.

'Butterflies will spread their wings,
Carla, when it is time, whether you
are there to see them or not.'

'Anyone who lives in this place must
feel the effect of it,' Steve put in mildly.
'There is something about this bay. I
think perhaps it's magic. I think, too,
I'll have some more coffee. Anyone
else?' His hand offered the coffee pot.
'Wasn't the airport coffee terrible?'

His voice rambled on, but it had
had its effect. Carla visibly took a
grip on herself. Paul's hands, which
had been whitening at the knuckles,
unclenched. The conversation veered
back to general topics and finally to
writing.

'I've got the script ready for you to
look at,' Janet said shyly. It was almost
the first remark she had uttered.

'Splendid,' Carla said, cooly. 'I'll
look at that in the morning. Tonight,
I think, an early night. Paul, I'd like to

speak to you before you go. You, too, Steve.'

Janet was dismissed. There was nothing for it but to leave them to it and go to her room.

She washed and changed for bed, but she could not rest. The murmur of voices, an occasional laugh, the chink of glasses from the dining-room downstairs haunted her thoughts. She felt alone and unhappy, pushed out from the charmed circle of which Carla was the centre.

She got up, slipped into a bathing suit, picked up a towel and went out into the warm, welcoming night. The water was refreshing, and as she stretched out under the starlit sky, floating on her back, her tensions disappeared.

Suddenly, on the water, a green glow broke the darkness. There was a splash, a gleam of green light, and then silence. Janet could feel her heart beat faster, and she lay motionless in the water, listening intently. For a moment all was quiet, and then there was a streak to her left. Once again, the unreal green light shimmered and died. Then to her right. Suddenly it was all around her, and as Janet watched, a small, dark shape leaped up into the darkness and fell back into a sea lit by magic lights. Something brushed her hand in the darkness. It felt cold and wet. Janet jumped, and at once the surface of the sea exploded into a river of lights. She gave a startled cry.

A figure detached itself from the darkness, and began to swim swiftly towards her. At every stroke the sea danced with light. It was so unreal that Janet could only close her eyes, half hoping it was a dream. The sea lapped cool against her body and her eyes snapped open to see the approaching swimmer, the amazing light on the water. It was all true. She panicked, struggled and began to sink.

The swimmer was beside her. Strong arms lifted her, and an American voice said, 'Hi, there. Take it easy. It's Janet,

136

isn't it? Seems like every time you and I run into each other I scare you real bad.'

'Joe?' she spluttered. 'What are you doing here?'

There was a soft laugh in the darkness. 'I came down here, because Elena's up there. And it sure is a nice night for a swim. All this phosphorescence.'

'That's what it is?' Janet said. 'Paul told me about it, but I've never seen it until now. What causes it?'

'Search me, but it sure is pretty.' He waved his hand across the surface of the water. It left a trail of light. 'Magic.' Another plop and a splash. 'And see that fish. Look at him go.'

Janet felt rather embarrassed. 'It's all so peculiar, so strange.'

'But kinda beautiful, wouldn't you say?'

Janet looked about her and now that her fears were calmed, she too fell under the magic spell of that enchanted sea. 'Beautiful,' she breathed. 'The sort of thing money can't buy.'

'Like happiness?' Joe said bitterly.

Janet felt uncomfortable. After a pause she said, 'I told Elena I'd seen you.'

'You did? Perhaps you shouldn't have done that,' Joe said softly, but he seemed pleased. 'What did the little lady say?'

'I told her you have been coming to the cove to find her. She was delighted.'

'She was?'

'She seemed surprised that you really cared about her.'

'I can't figure that out. I must have told her a hundred times.'

'It was her father, I think, who persuaded her that a rich American couldn't seriously love a young, Greek girl. And when her sister died . . .'

'Ah,' was all Joe said, but there was a world of meaning in his voice.

'I think that maybe I should get back now. It's getting late and — and I've got a busy day tomorrow.'

'I'll swim back with you,' Joe said, and together they struck out for the jetty. He pulled her up beside him, and wrapped the towel gently around her.

'Good-night, Janet,' Joe said softly. 'And thanks a million for talking to Elena.' He leaned forward and kissed her forehead lightly. 'I don't rightly know what's on your mind, Janet, but I kinda hope it sorts itself out, too. Anything I can do anytime, you let me know.' He pressed her hand and dived softly back into the black and silver sea and swam away.

An icy voice broke the stillness of the night. 'If you have quite finished your moonlight meetings, you'd better come in and get dry. You'll catch your death of cold if you stand there.'

Janet wheeled round. Paul was standing right behind her, and even in the moonlight, she could see that his face was like thunder.

# 7

'I came to find you,' Paul said coldly, 'because I thought you might feel left out. I see I needn't have worried. You've obviously found your own entertainment.'

'Entertainment?' Janet was puzzled.

'I'm sorry,' Paul said, 'perhaps that wasn't very polite. The young man I saw you with. I didn't mean to intrude. However, I think it would be better to avoid catching a chill.' His voice was like ice.

Realisation dawned. 'You saw Joe kiss me.'

'I'm very glad I did, under the circumstances. Do you know, I was seriously thinking of asking you to marry me.'

'Paul!' Her voice was anguished. 'I'm sorry — '

'There is no need to apologise,' he

140

said frostily. 'It's perfectly natural, after all. A young woman, a young man, a moonlit evening. Very romantic. I had thought that you were a young woman a little different from the average. I didn't think I would find you kissing some Greek stranger, but that was my mistake. You have nothing to apologise for. You may kiss anyone you choose.'

'He wasn't Greek — and he wasn't a stranger. I tried to tell you — '

Paul's outburst was angry. 'Of course not. No, not a stranger. He wouldn't be, would he? An arrangement, was it? I should have guessed.'

'No it wasn't,' Janet stammered. 'It wasn't like that at all.'

'No-one would just swim into the bay by accident,' Paul went on. 'The only reason for coming here would be to meet someone from the house.'

'Paul, I didn't even know I was going to go for a swim. Carla might have needed me. Anything.'

Paul stopped and looked at her. 'That's right. You couldn't know. So he came here, swam all the way around the bay, just on the off-chance.'

'No,' Janet said with a sob. 'That is, yes.'

'Very clear, my dear,' Paul said in a glacial tone. 'No, that is yes. However, it does put a new complexion on the matter. I thought we were dealing with a casual flirtation. It seems I was wrong. It looks like a case of real love, at least on his side. I owe the young man an apology.' His voice shook slightly, as he added, 'Does he know he is only one of a wide circle of acquaintances with whom you are on kissing terms?'

Janet's eyes had filled with tears, and her heart was too full for speech.

'Never mind,' Paul rushed on, filling the silence. 'Any man who swims around the bay at midnight just in the hope of seeing his lady love deserves all the support he can get. I can at least make his life easier by bowing out.'

Janet found her voice. 'I wish you'd listen!' she said frustratedly.

It was so unexpected that Paul stopped, shocked. 'I'm listening.'

'There is an explanation.' Janet shivered, half from cold and half from emotion. In an instant, Paul had wrapped the towel around her, his hand brushing her shoulder, her hair. Then he pulled away abruptly.

'Explanation?' he said, his voice tense. 'No explanation is necessary.'

'But it is,' Janet insisted. 'Paul, have you heard of Joe Winterbourne?'

'The American millionaire? Yes, of course I have.'

'Did you know that Elena was in love with him?'

'No, I didn't. I knew there was a flirtation with somebody — '

'It was no flirtation, Paul. The young man in the bay tonight was Joe Winterbourne. And he came on the off-chance of meeting Elena, not me.'

'He seemed easily distracted,' Paul observed bitterly.

'Please, listen, Paul. That boy has come to the cove every day for months in the hope of seeing Elena. He swims here every night hoping to glimpse her.'

'But he kisses you.'

'Only because I told him what he wanted to know, that Elena still loved him. You can't imagine how pleased she was when I told her I'd seen him.'

'So you had met before?'

'Well, yes, by accident,' she said. 'Sit down and I'll tell you the whole story.'

When she had finished, Paul said softly, 'I didn't know about this. I'm sorry, Janet. When I saw him kiss you, I suppose I was too jealous to think.'

'It was only a friendly kiss,' Janet said.

They talked for a long time before walking back to the house together, hand in hand in the silver moonlight. They had just entered the dining-room when, suddenly, the door burst open and Carla stood there, a wine glass in one hand. She turned her head and her magnificent, red hair gleamed in the lamplight.

'Well,' she said at last. 'If it isn't love's young dream. Do you think it's quite proper for you to conduct a torrid flirtation with my secretary, Paul?'

'Proper, Carla? And what exactly do you mean, proper?'

She gazed at him, the grey-green eyes defiant. 'You know exactly what I mean, Paul. Don't play games with me.'

Paul returned her look, coolly. 'I'm not sure that I do know, Carla. And I'm sure that Janet doesn't understand at all. Why don't you explain it clearly?'

Carla said nothing, and after a little, her eyes dropped.

'Besides,' Paul went on, 'it's hardly a flirtation. I was about to ask Janet to marry me.' His arm tightened around Janet's waist as he spoke.

'Paul, you can't do that. You can't.' The lofty, cutting disdain was gone. 'Paul, you can't do that to us.'

The 'us' went into Janet like a knife.

'Carla,' Paul said, and his voice was kinder, but firm and decisive. 'Carla, I know it's going to hurt you, but you will have to face up to reality. It's no good. I can't keep this life up for ever. It's all pretence.'

'What have you pretended?' Carla demanded. 'Have I ever asked you to say anything that wasn't absolutely true?'

'No,' Paul admitted. 'But there are things you've insisted on leaving unsaid.'

'You know why!' Carla almost spat at him.

'Of course I know why. I even understand, I think. I know what all this means to you, but I have a right to my own life — '

'Even at the expense of other people's?'

There was a pause, and then Paul said softly, 'Ask yourself the same question, Carla. Have you got the right to your own life at my expense? Or Janet's here? Or Elena and her

146

nice, young American friend? Carla, you can't go on interfering with other people's happiness in this way. This has to stop.'

'You'd risk all that we have worked for,' Carla asked incredulously, 'just to marry a secretary?'

'Not just any secretary,' Paul said. 'Only this one. I happen to love her.'

There was a deathly silence, and then Carla said abruptly, 'I think we'd better have a serious talk. As soon as possible. Tonight.'

'Ten minutes,' Paul said. 'I'll see you in the study.'

Carla stood for a long moment, and then turned back into the room. In the light the beautiful face looked tormented.

'I'm sorry, Janet,' Paul said gently. 'I should have spared you that.'

'It's all right,' Janet tried to say, but the only sound was a strangled sob.

Paul gathered her close to him. 'I seem to have been proposing to you,' he said at last. 'Darling Janet, will you marry me?'

She looked at him in the starlight. 'I'd like to, Paul, but — ' She screwed up her courage and asked the question she could hardly bear to utter. 'Paul, what about Carla?'

His arms loosened. 'What about Carla?'

'It seems to me she'll be very upset.'

'I'm sure she will, but she'll get over it. She'll see reason in the end.'

'Doesn't she still — is she very fond of you?'

'I suppose she is, in her fashion,' Paul said casually. 'I'm quite fond of her, come to that. Is it important?'

The nonchalance of his words shocked Janet. She said passionately, 'Of course it's important. You're important to her.'

Paul laughed softly. 'I'm useful to her, certainly, and I think she likes me well enough. Though she isn't very pleased with me tonight, is she?' He paused. 'Still, who can blame her. Her

148

life hasn't been very easy lately. No, she's all right really, is Carla. We're very good friends.'

'Just good friends? Elena said Carla loved you very much.'

He looked perplexed. 'Elena said that?' There seemed to be genuine bewilderment in his eyes. 'I don't understand it.' Paul looked at her for a long moment in the moonlight. 'I'll get it sorted out. Trust me,' he said.

'I trust you,' Janet replied, and tried to believe that she meant it.

She went to her room and changed for bed, but she couldn't sleep. The confrontation with Carla had chilled her, and she felt shaky and trembly. I need a cup of coffee, she told herself, and went down to the kitchen to make it.

Steve came in and joined her, full of little anecdotes, the plane, London, the rain. Janet found herself going back in her memory to another life. Could she have left it so short a time ago?

'Well, I'm turning in,' Steve said at

last. 'In the morning, we'll have a look at that script.'

'I'll just wash these cups,' Janet said.

'Then I'll say good-night. Sleep tight,' Steve said lightly, and left the room. Janet refilled her coffee cup. Then she, too, headed for bed.

Perhaps that was how fate had ordered it, for as she stepped into the unlit corridor, she saw a man ahead of her in the shadows. Carla's study door opened. Carla stood there, ravishingly beautiful, her magnificent hair cascading over her shoulders. The man took a step towards her.

'Paul,' Carla murmured, and the words branded Janet's heart like hot iron. 'Paul, I'm sorry.'

'It's all right,' he said smoothly, and moved into the room, his hands outstretched to take hers, his voice gentle and strangely tired. 'I understand. It isn't easy for you, but it has to be faced.'

Carla's hands gripped his, as she

150

said, 'How much does she know?'

Janet stood, frozen to the spot, as Paul said flatly, 'Nothing.'

'Are you certain of that?'

'As certain as I can be. Elena said something, warned her off me — '

'So she should.' Carla's reply was crisp. 'But that's all? She doesn't know about — anything else?'

'No,' Paul said. 'It's been a bit close once or twice.'

'Swimming at midnight. That could be dangerous.'

'It hasn't happened before. I did ask her once not to wander around the villa at night when everyone was in bed. She thought I was up to something, but she's always done as I asked.'

'She thought you were up to something? What, for heaven's sake?'

'Goodness knows. I didn't ask. Probably thought I was a smuggler.'

Carla laughed softly. 'So, what do we do now?'

'You know what I want, Carla.' He moved nearer to her and she looked up at him with haunted eyes. 'You know very well what I want.'

Carla moved past him and closed the door. Alone in the corridor, Janet stood in the darkness. She couldn't hear as much of their conversation now. Their voices were low, and the door thick, but snatches of it reached her ears.

'Marrying her . . . don't you think it's a good idea?'

'But what about me?' Carla was saying. 'What about us?'

Paul again. ' . . . absolutely necessary to stop it now. Otherwise it's going to go from bad to worse, and there's going to be all kinds of publicity. And that's the last thing you want.'

'All I wanted to do was live in peace and quiet with my husband.'

Silence. And then sounds that could only be muffled sobs. 'There, there,' Paul was saying. 'Don't cry.'

Janet could bear it no longer. Her imagination was painting pictures too vivid for comfort. Without caring who heard, she strode to her room, where she buried her head in her pillows, and cried herself at last into a fitful sleep.

When she awoke, it was to thoughts of Paul. 'Trust me,' he had said, and when he was with her she did trust him, implicitly. However, when she was alone, the doubts began to appear. How could she doubt the truth of what Elena had told her? Janet sat up in bed. Something just didn't add up. Something, somewhere was desperately wrong.

In her turmoil she had failed to close the shutters, and a shaft of moonlight was falling across her bed. I'll just close them, she thought, and go back to sleep. Tomorrow, whatever the consequences, I'm going to talk to Paul. If he can explain everything, that's fine. If not, I'll have to go back to London. She was astonished at how much the idea of leaving Spetse tugged at her heart. 'Tomorrow,' she repeated, firmly, half-aloud.

It was when she had one hand on the

shutter that Janet stopped. Something was wrong. She listened intently. The light wind rustled the olive leaves, and cicadas laughed in the warm, night air. Could she, dimly, catch the murmur of voices? She could not be sure.

Then, suddenly, it came to her. Through the open shutters came the unmistakable smell of cigarette smoke. Half-afraid to look, she craned her head and gazed down on to the patio. Carla was sitting there, her fur wrap around her shoulders. Her cigarette glowed, and the smell of smoke reached Janet afresh.

Carla! Of course! Why hadn't Janet thought of Carla and her perpetual cigarettes? Then her eyes moved to the balcony rail, and she shut them quickly with a stifled sob.

He was there, and as she stood and watched, he moved from the rail and came towards Carla. He took her in his arms and kissed her, hungrily.

Then Carla spoke, her voice muted and low. 'Darling,' she was saying, 'it's all been for you, you know that. I love you.'

His voice, strained and distorted with emotion, nothing more than a whisper, 'And I love you, Carla. Always, only you.' And their lips met again.

Janet closed her eyes and steadied herself against the window, gulping for breath, too stunned even to cry.

Then Carla's voice came again. 'Janet's got to know the truth, my darling. I know it's not what we planned, but after all — '

'My love.' His voice sounded strange, tense and deep. 'I'll come tomorrow and we'll tell her. She seems nice. I'm sure she'll understand.'

'She's upset. She doesn't know — '

He laid his finger on her lips. 'She'll forgive me when she sees me. Now, let me kiss you. I've been waiting a long time for this — '

Janet sank back from the window, and sat down heavily on the bed. For more than an hour she sat there, stupefied, her mind blank. When at last she moved back to the window, the patio was empty.

With trembling hands she closed the casement, and pulled the shutters together. Then she switched on the light, and took her battered suitcase from under the bed. Silently, she packed her possessions. For a moment, her glance rested on the beautiful dresses Paul had bought her, but she moved them gently and left them hanging in the wardrobe. She tied her hair into the once-familiar plait, slipped her coat over her shoulders, lifted her suitcase, and closing the villa door behind her, disappeared into the warm, Greek night.

# 8

The walk up the hill, which had seemed so magical on a warm afternoon with Paul at her side, seemed bleak and mysterious in the first glimmers of dawn.

It would be some hours before Janet was missed, but come breakfast time her absence would be discovered. She had left no note, no explanation of her sudden departure. She had been too distraught. Carla should at least have her resignation. She refused even to think about Paul.

Then, she must get away, but how? A boat would leave early this morning, and she could be in Athens by the evening, but what then? She had no air ticket, no job, no money to speak of. Ironically, if she had waited another day, she would have had money when Carla paid her, but, as it was, she had only a few pounds in the world. For a moment her resolution quivered.

There was a lump in Janet's throat as she continued up the path. The sun touched the hillside, stirring a thousand creatures into whirring flight. A thin warmth reached her through the branches, and deepened, even as it came. She climbed on, the suitcase heavier at every step, until she stood on the brow of the hill and looked down on Spetse town.

The town was already stirring. Little boats were landing their catch. The sturdy clop-clop of the harnessed horses rose from the narrow streets, and the thrum of a motor-bike hung in the air. In a field a man was working, whistling as he went. Out on the placid waters, the ferry was heading out across the bay.

Janet's heart sank. The ferry was the only cheap way of getting any distance. Her mind raced. Perhaps a little boat to the mainland. She could find out. She set out again, downhill now, and an hour or so later she was picking her way between the first houses on the outskirts of the town.

The sun was quite high by now, and it came to her that she was very thirsty. She counted her money. It was not a great deal, but it was enough. She would starve later. She walked boldly into a café and ordered coffee and rolls.

'You tourist?' the waiter asked, eyeing the suitcase as he served the coffee.

'Yes,' Janet said. 'I'm on my way home.'

'You like Spetse?' he wanted to know.

'Like crikey,' Janet said softly, unconsciously echoing Elena's words.

'Huh?' he said, and then, 'You American?'

'No,' Janet said, but even as the word left her lips, an idea came to her. 'But I have an American friend near here.'

'Yes?' the waiter said interestedly. 'You got his address?'

'No,' Janet said, coming back to the present. 'But he's well-known round here, I think. Winterbourne. Joe Winterbourne.'

The waiter put down the coffee cup with a clatter. 'Mr Winterbourne? You're a friend of his?' He looked at her with a certain incredulity.

'Yes,' she said, smiling uncertainly. 'You know him?'

'I know his house. My cousin who own this café show me.' He whistled. 'Sacristi! Is a big house he have there.' His young face crinkled in alarm. 'But, Mr Winterbourne is rich man. Maybe he don't like I tell you where he live.'

'You're quite right,' Janet said. 'He might not like it. But will you take him a letter from me?'

The boy looked hesitant. 'I go,' he said at last. 'When you want?'

'What about now?' Janet suggested. She opened her purse and offered him a tip so handsome he exclaimed involuntarily, 'Hey, maybe you are a friend of his.' He disappeared into the interior for a moment, and came back whistling. 'I in charge here, while my cousin in Corinth,' he said jauntily. 'They bring you more breakfast. I go.'

The fresh plate of rolls was better than the first, and she ate mechanically. The bill, when it came, was more than she had budgeted for.

'Don't you worry about that,' a soft American voice said. Joe Winterbourne was standing beside her. 'I'll get it. You just come along with me.'

The waiter was right. Joe Winterbourne's house was big, charming and gracious. Paul would have approved, Janet thought, and she winced.

'It's nothing special,' Joe said, when she admired it. 'But I'm glad you like it. You think Elena would go for it?'

Janet nodded glumly. 'I think that she'd love it here, Joe.'

'Well then,' Joe said, 'you sit yourself down over there, and just tell me what I can do for you.'

Janet looked at him in despair. 'It's — it's — ' The tears came again.

'A fella?' Joe enquired helpfully.

'Yes,' Janet said quietly. 'A fellow. I fell in love with a man, and I thought he loved me, but it turned out that he was married.'

Joe looked at her for a long moment. 'Would that be the same fella you were worried about before, that time we sat talking on the rocks? The fella you thought was plumb ignoring you one moment, and friendly as pie the next?'

Janet nodded.

Joe made a face. 'Well, it's none of my business, but seems to me maybe you know the reason he was acting kinda strange. Seems like maybe he had doubts which lady he was feeling for.'

'I thought so, too,' Janet said, 'until last night.'

'What happened last night?'

'I saw him with the other lady.'

'Oh.' There was a long silence, and then Joe said, 'Well, you just tell me what I can do to help. Do you need money?'

She flushed. 'Only a loan, Joe. I haven't the money for my fare home.' Her voice broke. 'Once I get back to England, I can send it back. I just want to get away without being found.'

Joe smiled. 'No problem. You want a ticket, I'll get that for you, no sweat. And don't worry about the money. Take it as a peace-offering for my having kissed you twice, without being invited.' His boyish face lit up. 'I'll sure be pleased to be able to do something to help. Anyone in trouble from that villa is owed a favour from me. You got money to live on just now?'

Janet told him how much she was carrying. 'It's enough, I think,' she said, 'Just until I can get a ticket.'

Joe looked at her steadily. 'Enough,' he said. 'Yes, if you live on cheese and tomatoes, and if you walk most of the way to Athens. Now, listen here. Seems to me there is only one way to deal with all this. It so happens that I have to go to Piraeus, pretty near straight off, to do some business. Strikes me you couldn't do better than to lie low here for a day or two. I'll sort out your airline ticket, and bring it back to you. That way you've got no worries about paying accommodation. You'd be doing me a favour, staying here to keep an eye on the place. There's plenty of food in the fridge, so there wouldn't be any call to go out into the town. This is a very small island, and news travels mighty fast.'

'Thank you Joe. It's really awfully good of you,' Janet said gratefully.

Joe grinned. 'Pleased to help out anyway I can.' He took a roll of notes from his pocket. 'That's for expenses this end. No, don't argue. You worry about that when you get to England. Right now, you need some money. Next thing, if I'm going to get me to Piraeus and get you this ticket all signed and sealed, I'd better get moving. There's a ferry sets off from here tonight I can catch. That way I'd be back on Thursday, easy. I'll try to get you a flight out next weekend.'

'I'm putting you to a lot of trouble.' Janet guessed that the trip to Piraeus was largely an excuse, so that she would not feel embarrassed at sharing his house. The thoughtfulness touched her, but Joe would have none of it.

'I've got to go, in any case. And it's easier to book an airline ticket there, anyway. I'll pop in at the café before I go and fix it so that Nicholai brings you fresh milk and bread every day. He won't talk.'

Janet said suddenly, 'Joe, there's another thing. I didn't leave any message or anything. I want to write some notes. Could you possibly see to it that they are delivered?'

'Why, sure thing,' Joe replied. 'Nothing easier. You want I should take them now? I've got to go book for the hydrofoil tonight. Here, there's pen and paper on that desk. You write your letters right now. I'll go fix some coffee.'

Janet sat at the elegant table and began by writing to Carla.

165

*Dear Mrs Ryder,*

*I have decided to resign my position as your secretary. Your manuscripts are typed and awaiting you in the study.*

*You will understand that my reasons for leaving are purely personal, and after our discussion last evening I am sure that you will agree that this is probably for the best. I am sorry to leave you at such short notice, but there seemed to be no other honourable solution. I do not, therefore, expect any part of the salary which should have been due to me.*

The second letter was harder to write.

*Paul,*

*I think you should know that I accidentally saw you and Carla on the patio last night. In the circumstances, you will understand why I have left the villa. I hope you will be very happy together, and I apologise for any distress I have unwittingly caused to either of you.*

She re-read the letter several times and then added,

*P.S. I have left your dresses in the wardrobe. Janet.*

To Elena she wrote a short note.

*You were quite right, Elena. I was wrong to love Mr Paul and Miss Carla was upset, as you said. Now that I know that, I have gone away. I am sorry I cannot say goodbye to you, except in this letter.*
*I spoke to Joe Winterbourne again. He is a good and kind man, and he loves you. Try to see him again, and find your own happiness. There is too much sadness in the world. Love, Janet.*

When Joe came back with the coffee she showed him the third letter. 'I hope you don't mind,' she said.

'It'll be a pleasure delivering it, ma'am,' he said.

'You can't go all the way round to the villa,' Janet said sharply.

'Why not?' Joe asked simply. 'I go there most days. Any case, it might not be necessary. Look.'

He gestured towards the window. Janet looked out at the harbour. There, nosing into the quay was the motor-boat, and even at this distance she could recognise Georgios slipping ashore with the mooring lines. There was a tall, dark figure at the helm. Janet took a deep breath. Paul was in Spetse town.

'Looks to me,' Joe said, 'they're mighty anxious to find you.'

Paul was off the motor-boat and walking along the quay, looking closely at the small crowds collecting to catch the next ferry. A small ferry pulled out for Kosta, and he hailed it and leaped aboard, as the gap between boat and shore widened. On the quayside, Georgios stood for a moment, undecided, then Janet distinctly saw him shrug his shoulders, and disappear into the waterside taverna. The ferry disappeared across the bay.

'Where's he going?' she wondered aloud.

'Nowhere,' Joe said. 'I thought you'd figured that. He thinks you might be on that ferry, or the last one, and he's gone to Kosta to find out. Strikes me he didn't want you to get away that easy.' He looked at her soberly. 'You sure you don't want to see him, talk it over a little? Seems to me he's kinda keen for a man who is in love with someone else.'

Slowly, Janet shook her head. 'I don't want to see him,' she said decisively. 'Not ever.' Suddenly, the lack of sleep and the unhappiness of the last few days overwhelmed her. The hand that held the coffee cup trembled.

'Come along,' Joe was saying. 'It's about time you got some sleep. Reckon I'll go down and book my ticket, and

I'll get these letters away, too.' He pushed open a door. 'This is the spare bedroom. Try to get some sleep.'

'I'll lie down,' Janet said. 'But I shan't sleep.'

But she did. When she woke, some hours later, she found Joe beside her, a steaming cup in his hand.

'Hey. Wake up, Cinderella,' he said, setting it on the bedside table. 'English tea,' he said again. 'I hope it's OK. I haven't rightly got the recipe.'

It wasn't very good, but Janet sipped it gratefully.

'I hope you like spaghetti bolognese,' he said. 'It's all I can cook. And you don't want to go out into the town.'

'Still there?' Janet asked.

'No. He's gone.' Joe frowned. 'You know, he actually spoke to me this morning. Told me to come and visit Elena if I wanted. Asked me if I knew you.'

'And what did you say?'

'I said yes, as a matter of fact I did. I said you were a real good friend of

170

mine, if it was any business of his.'

'And what did he say?'

'He said he guessed it were none of his business, but he thought he had a right to know seeing as how he'd asked you to marry him last night.'

'That's right.'

'Janet,' Joe said, sitting down, 'that fella is one very strange man. He came right out with that, right there in the street. Seems like he must have meant it.'

'But, Joe, he's already married. You told me that yourself. It was all in the newspapers and everything.'

'You quite sure he's still married?'

'Joe, I know what I saw and heard last night.'

Joe's face cleared. 'Sure you do. Well, that's all right then. I had it in my head maybe I shouldn't have said the things I did. He seemed kinda sincere, somehow.'

'What did you say, Joe?'

'Why, I came right out with it, and said it seemed to me that when a lady upped and left of her own free will, then he had his answer to his proposal. And he said, yes, he guessed so, but he seemed sort of shaken. Then he asked me if I'd seen you.'

'And you said no?'

'And I said yes, I had. You were in Nicholai's café this morning, I told him, but you weren't there now. I didn't exactly say it out loud, but I kinda suggested that maybe you caught the ferry first thing. I hope that was the right thing to do.'

Janet smiled, a mixture of gladness and pain. 'You've been splendid, Joe. No-one could have been nicer. And he's gone home now?'

'No,' Joe said. 'The boat's gone, but that young man went to Athens on the next hydrofoil. He must have stood all the way there, as there wasn't a spare seat to be had. I guess he'll either be hanging round the airport, or coming back home again by now, thinking he missed you. Mind you, I wish he'd told me I could go see Elena before I gave those letters to the baker to deliver.' He paused. 'Reckon I'll go up there soon as I get back from Piraeus.' He sighed. 'Maybe I'll even telephone from Athens.'

When Joe had gone, the house seemed strangely empty and horribly quiet. She stood by the windows and watched him go down to the quay, and make his way purposefully towards the ferry. She watched until only the wake shimmered and died in the still waters of the bay.

She watched until evening came, and even then, sat at the window and gazed as a solitary, horse-drawn, taxi carriage stood beside the water's edge, a black silhouette against the golden ripples of the sunset sea.

At last she moved away. Then she went to the spare room, and slept, rather to her own surprise, until the sun crept through the unfastened shutters and woke her to another day.

She lay there for most of the morning, thinking, until a rap on the door startled her. She got up quickly, and flattened against the wall of the bedroom, close to the window. The unseen figure at the door knocked again. Janet stood, pinned by panic, unable to move. Who could it be? No-one knew she was here.

The knocking ceased and Janet heard the sound of footsteps moving along the narrow, stone path which led around to the rear of the house.

The door of the back veranda opened with a squeak. Janet waited with a kind of panic for the sound of the key in the inner door. There was a scuffling noise, and then the footsteps again, retracing the path back to the front gate and the street.

Janet waited a full five minutes before she made her way cautiously to the back door. Through the glass she could dimly see something on the veranda. She unlocked and opened the door. In the shadows lay a cardboard box containing milk and a small, round loaf. It was still warm.

Janet let her breath out in a long, relieved rush. Of course! The boy from Nicholai's café. Joe had said he would come! She broke the warm bread and buttered it, and looked vaguely out at the harbour. What she saw almost caused her to swallow her breakfast in a single gulp. The motor-boat was back. Georgios was sitting in the deckhouse reading a newspaper and Paul was pacing the quay, looking anxiously at the face of every passer-by. They were still looking for her.

The next day passed in much the same way. This time, the bread had poppy seeds, and there was a sticky cake, tasting of honey and almonds. She watched the quayside, but the motor-boat didn't appear. The day dragged dismally, and evening seemed a long time coming. Night, when it fell, brought no relief and Janet lay wakeful, watching the sky change from black to ink, from indigo to blue, from blue to sapphire.

She began to feel a real hunger

for human company, and when the footsteps arrived on the third day, she was dressed and ready.

When she opened the door, however, the smile died on her lips. The young man in front of her was not the boy from the café. Janet could not place where she had seen him.

'Miss Lister?' the boy was saying hesitantly. 'Please, I have for you a message.' He paused dramatically. 'You know Elena, I think?'

Janet nodded.

'She my sister. She send me. She tell me I find you here.'

Janet shook her head in disbelief. They had found her!

# 9

The boy blinked dark eyes at her. 'Is OK. I am Yannos. I am brother to Elena. Elena is friend of Mr Winterbourne. Mr Winterbourne live in this house.'

'I was expecting the boy from the café,' Janet said, and realised it sounded aimless. 'He brings me milk and bread.'

Yannos shook his head patiently. 'No. You do not understand. I start again. I am Yannos. I am brother to Elena. Elena is one time friend to Mr Winterbourne. Then my father say is no good.'

Janet was herself again. 'Yes,' she said. 'I know. Joe Winterbourne was very upset about it. He really did love Elena, you know.'

'OK,' Yannos said brightly. 'Is true, and I think Elena all the time like him.'

'I'm sure of it.'

'Then you go, and when your letter comes she cries to me on the back of my motor-bike all the way to Spetse town. She come for seeing Mr Winterbourne, but next thing, there he is gone. She see him gone on this ferry before even she can speak to him. She cried to me all the way back to home. Even she forgets for buying the lamb for Miss Carla's dinner.'

Despite herself, Janet smiled.

'Is not for smiling,' Yannos said urgently. 'But yesterday, in the afternoon, came a telephone for Elena from Piraeus. Is Mr Winterbourne.'

'And Joe told Elena I was here?' Janet said, suddenly seeing the light.

'Oh, yes,' Yannos agreed. 'Elena tell to Mr Winterbourne how sad she is for you going suddenly away, and Mr Winterbourne explain her where you are and why you go.'

Janet looked searchingly at Yannos, but he smiled back at her, with an air of innocence. 'No good to look at me.

Elena don't tell me nothings, but you asking me, I think she is angry with him for tell you about Miss Carla marry Mr Stavropolous. She gave him — what is the English — part of her brain?'

'A piece of her mind,' Janet translated.

'Yes,' Yannos went on. 'And more she talk to Mr Winterbourne, more she upset. You say Joe tell you Mr Paul is married, now Joe say he don't know nothings about it.'

Janet started. 'Well of course he told me. How else would I have known about it. What is Joe playing at?'

Yannos was still trying. 'Please you come back with me,' he said. 'Elena very upset. She say me to come here for find you, and ask you please to come back and talk. Miss Carla upset, Mr Steve upset, Mr Paul very upset.'

'Very upset, I dare say,' Janet said bitterly. 'But there's no point in my coming back. I know all about it.'

'What you know, exactly?' Yannos said, the smile fading.

'I know that Carla is married to Mr Stavropolous, that they still love each other, whatever the public view is supposed to be. And I know this, too. I don't know what games are being played up there, but I know that between them Carla and her precious husband have made me very unhappy.'

There was a long silence. Then Yannos said, 'You won't come back?'

'Never. Though I suppose I might as well move from here now that everyone knows where I am.'

'Not everyone,' Yannos said. 'Only Elena and I.'

'Not Carla and Mr Stavropolous?' She could not bring herself to say Paul.

'Of course, no.' Yannos was genuinely surprised. 'If Elena cannot keep a secret, how long you think she work for Miss Carla and Mr Stavropolous?'

It was true. Elena had been very discreet. All the information about the Stavropolous household had come from Joe, not from Elena.

'In that case,' Janet said, 'I shall stay here. Thank Elena for me, but I shall not be returning to the villa.'

Yannos shrugged, a sad, dispirited Greek shrug. 'OK. If what you want, I tell her. We think that when you find out about accident, maybe is different.'

'Accident?'

Yannos looked at her with eyes from which the smile had totally vanished. 'You not hear about accident?' he said, shaking his head in disbelief. 'Surely you hear about that?'

'What accident?' Janet's hand felt for the doorpost, as though for support.

'Mr Stavropolous,' Yannos said. Then, seeing her face, he said, 'Is true. You don't know?'

'What happened to Mr Stavropolous?' Janet had to force the words out.

'Is his face,' Yannos said unhappily. 'Is all his face. Is the propeller from the motor-boat cut his face. Is terrible. Is doctor and nurse at the villa now for see what can they do for his face.' He broke off. 'Joe not tell you this?'

181

Janet shook her head impatiently. 'Wait,' she said, and disappeared into her room. When she came back she was carrying her handbag.

'Take me to the villa,' she said.

★ ★ ★

For the rest of her life, Janet was to remember that nightmare ride to the villa. Yannos boasted neither a helmet nor a pillion seat for Janet, but hustled her out on to the luggage carrier.

'You will hold on good,' he advised, twisting the throttle, and after that, all conversation was at a standstill. Clouds of dust rose around Janet's head, and got into her mouth and nose.

Every lurch of the bike was echoed by a sickening lurch of her heart as she thought of Paul. She had seen the propeller of the motor-boat, and she shuddered inwardly at the thought of the damage those blades could inflict.

The pace was furious, sliding sideways on every curve, but Janet, for all her fear, was mentally urging the bike farther and faster. Behind Yannos's broad shoulders, she managed, at last, to open her eyes momentarily. They were following a rough track which she did not recognise, until they breasted a small hillock.

There, nestling like a jewel among the olive groves, was the villa. The yacht bobbed at the quay.

There was no sign of the fateful motor-boat. Tears filled her eyes as she looked at the bay, and she had to fight a lunatic desire to scramble down from the motor-bike, and run to the villa on foot, as though this would somehow, magically, be faster.

'OK. You go in now,' Yannos said, stopping the bike. 'I see you later.'

He was gone before Janet had time to answer.

She was stiff and buffeted from her hectic ride, and it took her some minutes to walk down between the olives and the flowering shrubs to the patio.

Someone was sitting at one of the tables, a young woman with short, blonde hair. Janet had never seen her before. Carla's new secretary, already? As she drew nearer, she saw that the woman was, in fact, a nurse. Her thumping heart slowed a little. Paul could not be in danger then, if the nurse was sitting comfortably on the patio.

'Can I see Mr Stavropolous, please? Straight away?' she asked urgently.

The nurse looked at her, first in amazement, and then increasingly with interest. 'Are you Janet Lister?'

'That's right,' Janet said.

'Well,' the nurse said, getting to her feet, 'I guess it'll be all right. Elena said you might be back. You've had them all in a proper state. Even Mrs Ryder and Steve were quite worried about you. And Paul has talked about nothing else. I'm afraid everyone else has gone into Spetse town with the doctor in the motor-boat.' At the mention of the boat Janet winced.

184

'I'm surprised they're still using the motor-boat,' she faltered, 'after what happened. How is his face?'

'He's marvellous,' the nurse replied. 'Never complains, although it must be very uncomfortable. We'll do it, I think, eventually, but it'll be a long job I'm afraid. And I don't think he'll ever be free of it altogether. Come and see him then,' she said. 'I think he's well enough to talk now.'

She led the way into the villa and walked lightly upstairs. Janet's heart gave an unnatural lurch. The nurse was leading the way unhesitatingly to Carla's bedroom. The twin doors were both open, and Janet could glimpse the luxurious bathroom, and, on the other side, a white corridor, so clinical and tiled it could have been a hospital.

So much she saw, in a fleeting glance, but all her attention was focused on the figure propped in the great bed. The head was swathed in bandages, and the skin was drained of colour. The wavy, black hair hung in limp wisps across the pallid brow, and even the hands, which lay helplessly on the coverlet, looked somehow thinner.

He was asleep. At least, the one eye which remained uncovered by the bandages was closed, and the chest rose and fell with heavy, rhythmic breathing. Forgetting the nurse, Janet stole forward, and paused, gasping in horror. Below the bandages, the whole right side of the face was one terrible, hideous, disfiguring scar.

'Oh, my goodness.' The words were torn from Janet's lips, not loudly, but loud enough to hear. The pale eyelid fluttered open, and one dark eye, misted with pain, focused on Janet.

For a long moment they looked at each other, and then he spoke, in a harsh whisper. 'Hello, young lady. Who are you?'

She should have known, from that moment. Afterwards, looking back, she never understood why those words, breathed in a strange, cracked, distorted voice from the twisted lips, did not tell her everything. But she still persisted, too agonised by the dreadful purple scar where the flesh had been laid open to the bone, to think of more than the present moment.

'It's Janet,' she said. 'Janet, Janet Lister. Don't you recognise me?'

The figure in the bed stirred a little, uneasily, and then said, as though every word was torn from him in anguish, 'Oh, yes, Janet, of course. Please excuse me, so tired you know, and my eyes aren't used to so much light.' The voice drifted into silence.

'We gave him a sedative,' the nurse explained. 'He needs plenty of rest.'

The eyelid fluttered and lifted again. 'Just remembered — fault, yes — owe you an apology, my wife and I. Didn't want you to know — ' He paused. 'Didn't want you to know the truth, you know.'

She nodded dumbly, and turned away, unable to hide the tears which burned embarrassingly on her cheeks. She no longer knew whether she cried for herself or for the terrible catastrophe which had struck the man before her. Furthermore, she no longer cared. The nurse misunderstood.

'Now don't upset yourself, Miss Lister. Mr Stavropolous is making wonderful progress. We've been able to save the eye, and, given time we hope to be able to repair quite a lot of the damage. He's made a wonderful recovery so far.' She took Janet's arm, and led her outside again into the hot, sultry sunshine.

'It's a question of time,' the nurse was saying confidentially. 'Poor lamb. You should have seen his face when they first brought him ashore. It was hard to recognise that it was a face.' Janet shivered, but the nurse went on. 'His wife has been marvellous. It was his greatest fear, of course, that he would lose her affection.' She bent forward. 'It must be much worse for someone like that. They used to say that there wasn't a woman in the world who could resist him. A real lady-killer.

You can't imagine.'

'Oh, yes, I can,' Janet muttered huskily. Oh, Paul, Paul. At least, she comforted herself, he had the love of a beautiful woman, and, clearly, the best medical care that money could buy. She said as much to the nurse.

'Oh, yes,' the woman said, 'nothing's too good for him. Never has been. I don't think even he realised how much she has done for him.'

Janet sank down on the seat by the table where only a few short days ago she had breakfast with Paul in blissful serenity. She suddenly felt very old. The nurse was prattling on. 'She turned part of this villa into virtually a hospital, got the best plastic surgeons from Europe and America. And never gives up. Never. Right from the beginning she always believed something could be done.'

The words lapped around Janet like a dream. They made no sense. Turned part of the villa into a hospital — already?

'I don't understand,' she said stupidly. 'What don't you understand, Janet?' a familiar voice said. She whirled around. There was Carla, and Steve, and . . .

'Paul!' Janet just had time to see his face, as handsome and tender as ever, before confusion overcame her and she fainted at his feet . . .

\* \* \*

'How are you now?' Paul was asking. 'Drink this. It'll make you feel better.'

She sipped the coffee tentatively, not daring to allow herself to think, but revelling instead in his nearness and the wholeness of his beloved, familiar face.

'That's the second time,' Paul said, mock severely. 'We shan't let you go out on the patio if you keep fainting on us like this.'

'Don't tease me, Paul,' she said gently, and at once he was all contrition. 'Are you well enough for explanations?'

he said with loving concern. 'The nurse said you were not to be upset or troubled.'

'I won't be,' Janet assured him. 'In any case, I think I've finally worked out some of this for myself. Looking back on it, I seem to have been very dense.'

'You were not expecting it,' Paul said mildly.

'You are Paul Stavropolous, aren't you?' she said, wondering whether, even now, the jigsaw pieces were going to fit into place.

'Of course I am,' he replied, 'And the man in Carla's bedroom — '

'Is your brother. Of course,' Janet said. 'Who is married to Carla. I ought to have seen it before.'

'You ought to have trusted me,' Paul said in a low voice. 'I wanted Carla to tell you, but she refused point blank. We had quite an argument about it. Poor Carla, it meant so much to her and I owed them such a terrible debt.'

Janet sat up so quickly that her head spun. 'Debt, why?'

'Oh, Janet, there is so much to explain,' he said helplessly. 'Where on earth do I begin?'

'The accident?' Janet suggested. 'What happened?'

'It was a tragedy,' Paul said soberly. 'He almost died. Fortunately Georgios had turned off the motor by the time Phillip hit the water, and the blades had almost stopped spinning. Otherwise, I'm afraid, none of this would be happening. As it was, the damage was appalling. There have been ten separate operations to try to piece his face together, counting the one yesterday.'

'Can they . . . ?' Janet left the question unfinished.

'Patch as good as new?' Paul said, rather bitterly. 'No. But he will be at least presentable, not like something from a horror movie. If the papers had got hold of the story, you could imagine what would happen. We would have the bay crawling with photographers with telescopic lenses all trying to get pictures of the former screen hero. Carla was absolutely determined that nobody should know.'

'Some people must have known, surely,' Janet said.

'Well, scarcely anyone,' Paul said, 'outside of the family, and the medical staff. If there's one thing money can buy you in this world, it's privacy. Hardly any of the locals know.'

'Except Elena.'

'Except Elena,' Paul agreed. 'But she was as involved as any of us. It was her sister that Phillip dived overboard to rescue, you know. Her sister, Irene, my wife.'

'Your wife?' Janet echoed blankly.

Paul looked at her in astonishment. 'But surely Elena told you,' he said. 'I remember you speaking to me about it.'

Janet shook her head dumbly, 'But I thought — Carla — '

Paul gazed at her. 'You thought I

was married to Carla?'

'Joe told me that Carla was Mrs Stavropolous. What else could I think? And then I saw you with her on the patio — at least, I thought I saw you.'

Paul gulped. 'My poor Janet.'

'I tried to ask you,' Janet rushed on, 'and you said it was all over — ' A thought struck her. 'Is it all over?'

Paul's eyes were sad. 'Janet, my love, don't you know what happened to Elena's sister?'

Recollection dawned. 'She's dead,' Janet breathed.

'Oh, yes,' Paul said soberly. 'Phillip did his best, but her dress caught in the propeller. It was all over so quickly.' He shuddered.

'Oh, Paul,' Janet said. 'Did you love her very much?'

'Very much,' Paul said, and a wistful smile broke on his face. 'She was like the sea, Janet. One moment she was a raging storm, the next full of warmth and tranquillity. Even marrying me, you know, that was typical. Not what her family expected. She was an interior decorator, too. You know Carla's room? She designed that. Carla adored her, even to the extent of forgiving her for — for what happened.'

'It's a beautiful room,' Janet ventured.

Paul stared at her. 'Beautiful? It's preposterous! It's excessive. It's Irene all over. It's the way she lived, and the way she died. Insisting on standing on the foredeck in a howling storm, to feel the wind on her face, in her condition?'

Janet swallowed. 'You mean — '

'She was expecting our baby. I was mad with grief. If Phillip hadn't needed me, I don't know what would have happened. I had no interest in work, commissions, anything. I had more than enough to live on, and I just didn't care about the outside world. I hated the sea. I even felt I couldn't go on living.'

'I see.' Janet's voice was very small and strained.

'Carla kept coming and going, organising Phillip's medical care. She had a string of secretaries, but they were either incredibly nosy, or hopelessly flirtatious.' He smiled. 'But then one day you came along. I remember seeing you at the airport, so lost and alone, in your ridiculous grey coat and those great, big, stupid glasses on your nose, and I wanted to look after you. Then, when you began speaking to me in that idiotic fashion — ' He laughed. 'I laughed again for the first time in months, Janet. I loved bringing you to life, showing you the island. You were so warm, so unaffected. Everything was new and wonderful. I fell in love with you.'

'But Irene . . . ?' Janet faltered.

'Nothing can damage the memory of Irene,' Paul said gently. 'It was lovely, and it was precious, but it is over. With you, I feel I could pick up the pieces, and start again.'

'Oh, Paul,' Janet said.

He bent towards her. It was the last

thing she said for a long time . . .

It was Elena who interrupted them. 'I sorry, Mr Paul, Miss Janet — ' she said, and stopped. A huge smile creased the olive face. 'Well, Miss Janet, I very pleased to see you here.'

Janet did not let go of Paul's hand. 'And you'll forgive me, Elena, for taking your sister's place?'

Elena looked at Paul, and back to Janet. 'I sorry again, Miss Janet. In my country to lose a wife is very terrible, especially when is going to have baby. I think Mr Paul show no respect, and I very angry for that, but when I see that he love you proper, and he can get happy again, and I see you are real, nice lady, and also is long time since Irene die — '

'So the proper mourning period is over,' Paul observed briefly. 'I think that's probably the most important fact of all.'

'Any case,' Elena went on, 'I get happy for you and Mr Paul be friends. Now I get coffee.'

'What will happen to Phillip, now?' Janet asked, hardly liking to.

'Well, when the surgeons have finished with him, it should be possible for him to make a fresh start. Not in front of the cameras, perhaps, but behind them. He has great flair, my brother. Even before the accident he was interested in directing.'

'And will that be possible?' Janet said.

'Carla will see to it,' Paul said. 'She's seen to it already. She's sold the film rights of her new book, but only on condition that she can nominate the director.'

'Who will be Phillip?'

'Of course.'

'One thing I don't understand,' Janet put in, 'is why she insists on calling herself Mrs Ryder. If that's her maiden name, that is.'

'It isn't though,' Paul said laughing. 'Haven't you worked that out yet? Carla wrote her first two books under her own name. They sold very well,

198

but she didn't think it had a very romantic ring. Then Ryder Hall came up for sale, and she and Steve decided to buy it, so she adopted the name. She insisted on the 'Mrs' because it was the only way she could publicly remind herself that she was a married lady.'

'She and Steve bought the house,' Janet said unbelievingly.

'Well, he is her brother,' Paul said. 'Can't you see the likeness? He's always been her literary agent, right from the beginning. He was the one who got her the job writing the film script where she met Phillip.'

'Meanwhile, your sister-in-law acts as your housekeeper,' Janet said.

'She offered,' Paul said, 'after Irene's death. We weren't very happy about it at first, but Elena insisted. It was better to have a member of the family here. Phillip didn't mind Elena, and I wouldn't have been happy with any other woman here either. And her father didn't mind because — '

'Because you were family. I see.'

Janet squeezed his hand. 'I couldn't quite understand how Joe Winterbourne came to fall in love with someone's family servant.'

'Well, she isn't really a servant,' Paul said. 'Greek girls often help out in the house when there is illness or death. But her father wasn't a bit keen on poor Joe. He seems to feel that Irene's death was a direct result of her marrying 'above her station,' because she fell off an expensive motor-boat I suppose. He did his best to stop the romance, and between us, Carla and I were so anxious for secrecy we more or less cut poor Elena off from everyone but her family.'

Suddenly Janet began to laugh.

'What is it?' Paul said, half-laughing himself.

'I was just thinking of you all, closing ranks around Phillip. And it suddenly struck me that if Carla is Steve's sister — I can understand why she changed her name. Carla Trout isn't the best name for a romantic authoress, is it?'

'What about Janet Lister?' Paul asked. 'I don't think much of that name, either. Why don't you change it. Stavropolous now, that's a nice name, don't you think?'

'A beautiful name,' Janet agreed. 'I'll have to learn to spell it.'

'I'll help you,' Paul said. 'We'll think of something.' He took her in his arms again, and pressed his lips to hers.

A few minutes later, she said, 'This isn't helping me to spell.'

'Be quiet,' Paul said. 'You've just agreed to marry me. Now, concentrate.'

★ ★ ★

They made the announcement that evening at dinner.

'Well, let's toast the bride and groom to be,' Steve said, filling his glass. 'Paul and Janet. I can't say it's altogether a surprise, Janet. Paul told me when I rang that he was hoping to propose to you.'

'Of course, it was you!' Janet said.

'The conversation I overheard. I couldn't understand why Paul was saying the things he said.'

'What did I say, exactly,' Paul wanted to know.

'You said something about, 'she had ideas about settling down into married life and running the villa' and how you couldn't go on doing what she wanted for ever — ' Her voice tailed off. 'Oh, it all seems so simple now, but at the time you can't imagine what I thought.'

'Poor Janet,' Paul said. 'Everything seemed to conspire to give you the wrong impression of me. Carla's photograph — '

Carla laughed. The strain and tension had gone from her face, and she was so radiantly beautiful that Janet found it hard to believe that she was a real, breathing, living person.

'Oh, yes, that photograph,' Carla said. 'There was I, wanting a discreet secretary, and the first thing I catch her doing is looking at a photograph of

Phillip. I shouldn't have left it about, but I'd just been making arrangements with the surgeon and I felt so alone. I just had to look at his dear face.' She laughed. 'I nearly sacked her on the spot. I would have done it if hadn't been for Steve.'

'I've got a lot to thank you for, Steve,' Paul said with a smile.

Steve grinned. 'You nearly lost her though, you know, Paul. When she got that message that Phillip's operation would have to be postponed, and Carla decided to stay and find another surgeon. I almost had to carry Janet on to the plane.'

Janet grinned at the recollection. 'I thought you were all involved in something terribly sinister,' she said.

'And I didn't help,' Phillip said, 'lurking on the patio in the dead of night.'

'You certainly frightened me,' Janet said. 'This figure, hovering in the dark, smoking. I thought I was imagining it.'

'I didn't mean to alarm you,' Phillip said, 'but until this operation, I couldn't bear the daylight. I had to become a sort of nocturnal animal. There was one terrible night when you found us both on the patio. I left Paul with my ashtray — put him in a difficult situation, I'm afraid. But we hope, don't we,' he said, turning to the nurse, 'that this operation should do the trick.'

'The doctor says it's doing wonderfully,' the nurse said smiling.

'I was proposing a toast,' Steve said, 'to the bride and groom to be. Health and happiness.'

'I'll drink to that,' Phillip said. 'If it's only in orange juice.'

'To you, Janet,' Paul said, raising his own glass. 'To my sunshine.'

'There's only one flaw that I can see,' Carla said, joining the toast. 'No sooner do I find the perfect secretary than I lose her again.'

'I don't know.' Paul laughed. 'Seems to me you have the perfect set-up. Carla can write it, Janet can type it,

Steve can sell it, Phillip can direct it, and I'll design the sets.' They all laughed.

'And what about Elena?' Janet said.

'I think,' Carla said, 'that Elena has plans of her own involving Joe Winterbourne. Oh dear,' she teased, 'and I was just getting to like lamb.'

'Please, Miss Carla,' Elena said reddening, 'is time for me and Joe, but if you wanting someone to cook and look after house there is a cousin to me, called Lilli — '

'To Lilli,' Carla said gaily. 'To Elena and Joe, to all of us.' They refilled their glasses.

Elena moved closer to Janet. 'I think,' she whispered, 'you love Mr Paul and you love Spetse? Is true?'

'Is true,' Janet whispered back. 'Like crikey.'

We do hope that you have enjoyed reading this large print book.

Did you know that all of our titles are available for purchase?

We publish a wide range of high quality large print books including:
**Romances, Mysteries, Classics, General Fiction, Non Fiction and Westerns.**

Special interest titles available in large print are:
**The Little Oxford Dictionary Music Book, Song Book Hymn Book, Service Book**

Also available from us courtesy of Oxford University Press:
**Young Readers' Dictionary (large print edition) Young Readers' Thesaurus (large print edition)**

For further information or a free brochure, please contact us at:
**Ulverscroft Large Print Books Ltd., The Green, Bradgate Road, Anstey, Leicester, LE7 7FU, England. Tel:** (00 44) **0116 236 4325 Fax:** (00 44) **0116 234 0205**

# A SUMMER FOLLY

## Peggy Loosemore Jones

Philippa Southcott was a very ambitious musician. When she gave a recital on her harp in the village church she met tall, dark-haired Alex Penfold, who had recently inherited the local Manor House, and couldn't get him out of her mind. Philippa didn't want anything or anyone to interfere with her career, least of all a man as disturbing as Alex, but keeping him at a distance turned out to be no easy matter!

# IMPOSSIBLE LOVE

## Caroline Joyce

When Maria goes to live with her half-brother on the Isle of Man, she finds employment as a lady's maid to the autocratic Mrs. Pennington. Maria finds herself becoming very attracted to the Penningtons' only son, Daniel, but fights against it as he is from a different class. She becomes engaged to Rob Cregeen, who takes a job in the Penningtons' mines. But when Rob is killed in a mining disaster, Maria blames the Penningtons . . .

# THE DARK DRUMS

## Anna Martham

Anona Trent is engaged by Jermyn St Croix as governess to his daughter at his plantation home on the island of Saint-Domingue in the Caribbean. At Casabella, Anona discovers there is a secret connected with the death of Jermyn's wife, Melanie, and that Jermyn himself is cold and forbidding. Before long, Anona finds herself falling in love with a man who tells her he can never return her love, and on the exotic island she finds both mystery and despair.